A MESSAGE FROM CHICKEN HOUSE

Nicki Thornton won our *Times*/Chicken House Children's Fiction Competition with this lovely fantasy whodunnit. It has *all* the ingredients for a classic read: a mysterious old hotel in a wood, a lost and vital magical item hidden inside, strange magicians, an intriguing locked-room murder – oh, and a talking cat. Can you figure it out before our plucky hero?

**BARRY CUNNINGHAM**
Publisher
Chicken House

# THE LAST CHANCE HOTEL

## NICKI THORNTON

Chicken House

2 PALMER STREET, FROME, SOMERSET BA11 1DS

Text © Nicki Thornton 2018
Illustrations © Matt Saunders 2018

First published in Great Britain in 2018
Chicken House
2 Palmer Street
Frome, Somerset BA11 1DS
United Kingdom
www.chickenhousebooks.com

Cover and interior design by Steve Wells
Cover and inside illustrations by Matt Saunders
Typeset by Dorchester Typesetting Group Ltd
Printed and bound in Great Britain by CPI Group (UK) Ltd, Croydon CR0 4YY

The paper used in this Chicken House book is made
from wood grown in sustainable forests.

5 7 9 10 8 6

British Library Cataloguing in Publication data available.

PB ISBN 978-1-911077-67-1
eISBN 978-1-911490-41-8

*For my family,*
*Mark, Alex and Tim*

# REGISTER OF GUESTS AT
# THE LAST CHANCE HOTEL

Room 1    *DR TORPOR THALLOMIUS –*

*VIP guest, allergy to raspberries*

Room 2    *PROFESSOR PENELOPE PAPPERSPOOK –*

*likes to be woken by the sound of birdsong*

Room 3    *GLORIA TROUTBEAN –*

*a small desk for doing homework, room adjoining*
*Professor Papperspook*

Room 4    *DARINDER DUNSTER-DUNSTABLE –*

*3 extra-soft pillows*

Room 5    *ANGELIQUE SQUERR –*

*full-length mirror*

Room 6    *GREGORIAN KINGFISHER –*

*a room with a picture of people playing sport*

Room 7    *COUNT BOLDO MARRED –*

*no special requests at all*

# PART ONE

# 1. THE LAST CHANCE HOTEL

In the kitchen of the Last Chance Hotel the loudest sound you were usually likely to hear was the gentle bubble of a lone egg coming to the boil.

But today, the air was alive with yells from Henri Mould, the balding head chef, bent double with old age, barking out orders as he hobbled around the kitchen.

'Seth – those tarts! Out of the oven. Now!' yelled Henri, causing kitchen boy Seth to twist around on his spindly legs and hurtle to the other side of the kitchen. All around him, the air was filled with the smell of garlic butter and roasting meat, and cloudy with a dust of flour, herbs and spices. Steam ballooned, jellies set and saucepans bubbled.

If ever Seth Seppi wished he could be even the tiniest bit magic it was now. Because a spell to split himself into three was surely the only way he was going to get through all the tasks he'd been set by his three nasty bosses – crotchety Henri and the two owners of the Last Chance Hotel, snappy and spiteful Norrie Bunn and her oily, penny-pinching husband, Horatio. It felt like the hotel had been preparing forever for these special guests that Mr Bunn had been bouncing on his toes about, and today was the day they were due to arrive.

'I need more pepper. Quickly boy!' screeched Norrie Bunn from the stove, sending a long dribble of peppercorn sauce flying across the kitchen as she launched a dripping spoon in Seth's direction. Her long, brittle grey hair was tied back from her pointy face as she sweated over the sauce, trying not to sneeze.

At least the Bunns' monstrously unpleasant daughter, Tiffany, was at her posh chefs' school, far away from her favourite entertainment – tormenting Seth.

Mr Bunn burst into the kitchen flapping his hands and squealing, 'They're here! they're here!' like a small kid announcing Christmas, before rushing back out into the lobby.

Even more startling, Mr Bunn was wearing a cherry-red waistcoat and stripy trousers, rather than the familiar drab grey suit he had worn every day for years.

Norrie Bunn tugged off her apron and, smoothing down her long grey hair, rushed to attend to her guests in the lobby.

Seth managed to be the first to reach the crack in the kitchen wall where it was possible to see through to the lobby and sneak a glimpse of the arriving guests. As he put his eye to the hole, he could hear the sound of keys being jangled and Mr and Mrs Bunn, on their best behaviour, greeting the new arrivals.

Henri moved across the kitchen with unusual sprightliness, poked Seth out of the way with a very sharp elbow and peered through the crack. 'Is *that* our VIP guest, Dr Thallomius? The one we've put in all this hard work for? Not very impressive. All this work,' Henri groaned as he pressed his paunch tenderly, 'gives me gas.'

Seth had not expected their VIP guest to look like

a miniature Father Christmas. Dr Thallomius had white hair, a round tummy and eyes that twinkled, but he must have only come up to Seth's shoulder.

'And the chap with him – what a peacock.' Henri continued his spying. 'Guess that's his security he's insisted on bringing with him. Security! Looks about as good at security as a chicken. What a ridiculous moustache.'

'That'll be Mr Gregorian Kingfisher.' Seth had glimpsed a young man in a bright green, tight-fitting suit, with well-combed dark brown hair, a very large and luxuriant brown moustache and a sprinkle of freckles across his nose. 'He's the one who asked for a room with a picture of people playing sport.'

Guests often made special requests, but it was the first time anyone had been fussy about the artwork in their room. These guests were so fascinating. Seth had never known this many people staying. Probably because outside the hotel the whole world was nothing but never-ending trees. Seth could just about remember the days when the Last Chance Hotel had always been full. That had been when his father had been chef here. In those days, people had relished the challenge of travelling to so remote a place just for the reward of trying his famous cooking.

Seth longed for a summons from Mr Bunn that

someone needed help with their bags, so he could get a closer look.

'Can see why Thallomius wanted Miss Squerr along as his assistant,' growled Henri, turning his head and giving Seth a momentary chance to take another peek.

Angelique Squerr's head was held as high as if she was making an entrance to a grand audience of thousands. Her hair was long, straight and dark, except for one long section of red down the right-hand side. It looked as if it had been polished. A film star? Under the twinkling chandelier she made the clutter of well-polished wooden furniture and pictures in old frames seem faded and worn.

'Back to work, Seth,' snapped Henri, picking up a knife and heading to chop some vegetables. 'Or that washing up will reach the ceiling.'

But before Seth could make a start, Henri let out a cry and the knife in his hand fell with a clatter to the cool flagstones of the kitchen floor.

An insect flew past Seth's nose to batter against the window. Henri cowered.

'It's just a bug, Henri,' soothed Seth, gently teasing the little creature towards the open window. It looked like it was on fire, with a glowing phosphorescent tail.

'That's not just any bug.' Henri's eyes grew wide. 'That's a *luciole*. Do you know what that means?'

'You mean it's a firefly. Must have got lost from the glow-worm glade. It's beautiful, come and take a look. They look like magic, don't you think?'

'But it's inside!' Henri hissed, dabbing his sweating upper lip. 'In my country if a lightning bug flies in the window, it means – it means a *death*.' Henri gripped Seth's arm hard. 'Seth, someone is going to die.'

## 2. FISH HEAD SOUP

Seth worked his arm out from Henri's frightened grip. 'That's just an old legend, Henri, don't worry. No one is going to die.'

He released the firefly to freedom, but Henri picked up his whittling knife and scuttled off in a panic. It was left to Seth to take over preparing the vegetables for tonight's feast.

Whittling was what Henri did whenever he was stressed and Seth was used to coming across a parsnip that had been turned into a striding giraffe or a piece of wood fashioned into a cute fox cub. But why did it always happen just when he really needed Henri to be making a roast chicken or a steak and kidney pudding that was needed for dinner?

Seth scurried past the huge saucepan where broth was bubbling, ready for the fish heads to be added to the hotel's signature Fish Head Soup. The pile of fleshy fish heads Seth had prepared earlier were waiting, their eyes staring at him as though they were saying, *You think you've got it bad.*

He skidded to a halt.

His nose, taking in the aroma of stock and spices, was telling him something important. The broth wasn't quite right. And his nose was never wrong.

Seth carefully lifted one of the fish heads for Nightshade, the hotel cat. He slipped it into one of the many pockets of the bright blue tunic he wore under his apron. It might be rather gaudy, but the tunic was almost the only thing left to him by his father. That, and a mirror that was so useless sometimes it looked as if it was reflecting what happened in an entirely different room.

He took a tiny spoon, dipped it into the pan and brought the liquid to his lips. It was wonderful and warming and reminded him so much of his father, who was in danger of becoming little more than a distant memory.

Seth could recall him by a smell of cinnamon and spices and all those lessons, side by side, as they'd baked bread and made soup. He was left with his father being like a small glow of love inside of him, which was more memory than he had of his mother. Any thought of her made Seth's insides tighten from a sadness that she had died when he was just a baby, and he struggled to remember her at all.

Seth reached up to the shelf overcrowded with a mad jumble of bottles and jars of every imaginable shape, size and colour, took a pinch of some fine strands of dried yarrow and sprinkled them in, thinking that although Mr Bunn never tired of telling him how his father had been disgraced, he was never specific about exactly what he was supposed to be have done.

But Seth's father had come up with the recipe for the soup and with such important guests, Seth was going to make sure it would be served up perfectly. Chef Henri Mould always skimped on ingredients and never got the hotel's famous dish quite right. So, with a stealthy glance over his shoulder, Seth reached for the saffron in its long clear glass jar. His head swarmed with the repeated warnings from mean Mr Bunn. *'Use it very sparingly. Gram for gram saffron costs more than gold.'*

Seth took four tiny delicate strands of saffron between his fingers, shot another fearful glance over his shoulder and sprinkled them into the broth. He smiled as the soup turned a satisfying rich golden colour.

'Well, well, well, Seppi, you're *so* going to pay for that.'

Seth jumped, almost dropping the jar. There was no mistaking that hated voice. The last voice he had expected to hear today.

Tiffany Bunn, the hotel owners' odious daughter, was leaning smugly against the kitchen door frame.

## 3. It Might Be a Pudding

'Seth Seppi the saucepan scrubber. The worst kitchen boy in the world. Still here I see?' Tiffany's voice oozed with contempt.

'Tiffany!' Seth stammered, doing his best to sound casual as he tried to hide the jar of saffron behind his back. 'You're back early. School OK?'

Tiffany Bunn slouched against one of the kitchen cupboards and tipped her head to one side. 'Aw, you missed me. Dad summoned me back to this miserable place at the end of the earth. He's a total pain when he's stressing. He thinks I'm going to help. But, aw, sweet. I didn't realize you counted the days just like I do.' She gave a flick of her gloriously long blonde hair, the hair of an angel.

'I've really got to—'

'Aw, too busy to chat? And there's me just longing to see you after spending my days all *whisk this* and *fry that.*' She leant into him so close her high forehead almost touched Seth's shoulder. 'Chef school has taught me one really important thing. There is nothing more tediously boring than cooking.'

Seth's dearest wish was that one day his talent for cooking was going to be his way out of here. He longed to cook the sort of dishes that people would travel miles for. Just like his father. When Henri was occupied whittling, Seth grabbed every chance he could to experiment. Although sometimes, even in his dreams, he couldn't picture himself ever being anywhere else.

'Don't you want to know why coming back to this dump is bearable? Why I look forward to coming back?' Tiffany whispered.

Seth clutched the jar of saffron even tighter as she moved in so close he could feel her breath on the side of his neck, smell her long journey on her skin in a cocktail of train dirt mixed with the sweet whiff of hot chocolate and a bacon sandwich.

'It's seeing you, my little saucepan scrubber. Still up to your elbows in potato peelings and dirty pots? Some things will never change.' Her blue eyes opened hypnotically wide. Her skin was so pearly white, her smile so dazzling, it was easy to miss Tiffany's real danger – that she concealed just the right amount of brains to make her absolutely lethal. 'I long to come back because it is such fun to see exactly what sort of trouble I can get you into.'

She darted to grab Seth's arm from behind his back. She snatched the jar of saffron, twisting his arm painfully.

'But you do make it so very easy for me,' she purred. 'Stealing from the kitchens?' She laid a finger on the smooth skin on her cheek and her lovely face curled into a malicious smile. 'Now what are we going to do about that?'

'Tiffany – I can—'

'Shame I can't take that out of your salary, Seppi. Because you don't earn one, do you. We have to pay for all your food because your miserable good-for-nothing father disappeared and took some of my dad's most valuable possessions.'

Seth hated the way he let her words claw at his insides. But he was stuck here. He had nowhere to go – no friends, no relations. Sometimes he thought he'd be here for ever.

'Dad is still sadly deluded into believing I have an interest in sweaty ovens and cookery books at that lame school. Do my parents even care that they are totally ruining my life?' Tiffany took out a piece of folded paper and shoved it into Seth's hand, flicking his forehead with her middle finger. 'Still, I know you don't want to disappoint my dad.'

'What's this?' asked Seth.

'Something called a raspberry pavlova,' said Tiffany, checking her elaborately painted nails.

Mr Bunn delighted in challenging his daughter to come up with the most complicated dishes and boasted about how well she made them and how much she was learning at her posh school. But it was always Seth she made do all the work.

Seth tucked the piece of paper behind his ear. 'Sure, I'll look at it later.' The clock was telling him there were less than three hours to go until the important dinner. He slid some tarts on to a rack to cool. 'When d'you need it? We're kind of busy, you know, Tiffany.'

Tiffany raised her hands and stepped back. 'Sorry. My bad.' Then she leant in and yanked the piece of paper out from behind his ear. *'I'll look at it later,'* she mimicked with a low chuckle. 'Or how about you do it now?'

'Well, when do you need it?'

Tiffany's next words were almost drowned out by the loud sizzle and splatter as he put the potatoes into the oven to roast.

'It's for dinner tonight, obviously. I think it might be a pudding.'

Seth stopped and stared at her wide-eyed.

'Oh, I can't possibly do it,' she said, 'but let's hope you can, or else I shall be telling my dad about you pinching that saffron. And the fish head – don't think I didn't notice that. Snacking on raw fish heads now, Seppi.' Tiffany tutted and shook her head. 'Not a good sign. Or were you stealing it for that mangy cat you're so fond of?'

Seth took a deep breath. Tiffany always, within seconds, made his insides feel like they were tightening into such a fierce ball it made Seth picture making his hand into a fist and punching her right in the middle of those perfect teeth of hers. He swallowed it down. He smiled.

'I only put the saffron in the soup to make it taste like it's supposed to. That's not stealing. Your dad wants to impress these guests.'

Tiffany grabbed a handful of the tarts Seth had

just rescued. 'And if you're not careful you'll be blamed for these going missing as well. Unless, of course, you'd like to help me with the – what's it called again?'

'The pavlova?'

'That's it. And if we say, lemon-head, that if you manage to make the best pavlova the world has ever seen, then I might just be able to forget what I saw.'

Seth hesitated, looking at Tiffany's evil smile, and they both knew he had no choice. 'I might be able to – if you polish the candlesticks and lay the table.'

Tiffany responded with one of Seth's most hated sounds – her awful barking laugh.

'We both know that's not going to happen saucepan scrubber.' She tossed a piece of pastry in the air and caught it neatly in her upturned mouth. 'If you've got one or two things to do, I have a little word of friendly advice. Jolly well get a move on, and don't hang around here yakking.'

## 4. DR THALLOMIUS HIMSELF

A call went up from the lobby. 'More guests Seth.
Bags! Quickly! Get a move on.'

In response to Mr Bunn's summons, Seth moved
swiftly into the entrance lobby, where the crystal
chandelier twinkled an inviting party atmosphere
over the dark panelling. He only just stopped
himself skidding on the floor he'd finished polishing
at five that morning and narrowly avoided colliding
with an extraordinary-looking boy about his own
age.

The boy was dressed in a tight green velvet suit and his oversized grin and enormous pointy ears seemed to be doing their best to make up for the rest of him being undersized.

'Steady,' the boy said, flinging up his arms and spinning around on his surprisingly short legs, as if Seth had actually cannoned into him. Then his face cracked into a mischievous smile and he gave Seth a cheeky wink. 'No harm done.'

'Watch out Seth!' snapped Mr Bunn, clicking his fingers. 'Master Darinder Dunster-Dunstable needs help with his luggage, not to be sent flying into next Christmas. And ask Count Marred if he has a bag too.'

As Seth bent to pick up two huge bags, he eyed the hooded figure that towered next to Darinder, shrouded in a black travelling cloak that smelt of a long journey from a cold place.

The traveller flung back the hood, revealing a dark domed head, the skin hatched with wrinkles like a raisin, and a monstrous scar running from the bottom of his bulbous nose to the corner of his lip so it was lifted as if in a permanent sneer. It was much the same look as Tiffany achieved without needing the scar. Seth took a small, alarmed step backwards.

'Room Seven, if you need me, young man,' the cloaked count said cheerily to Darinder, heading for the stairs, his smile revealing missing and blackened teeth. He ducked to avoid the low ceiling as he began to climb the stairs. 'Can't believe old Torpor Thallomius himself is here. We've got catching up to do. Room One did you say?'

'Dr Thallomius himself is here?' repeated the boy, his eyes widening. 'Really?'

The heavy wooden front door creaked as it slowly swung inwards, announcing another arrival.

In strode an imposing woman who flapped towards them in a cloud of tropical perfume. She wore a huge tent-like dress of a hundred different hues, and took up more than her fair share of the hotel lobby. Her tower of blonde hair, streaked with colour, was piled so high on her head it almost scraped the low ceiling of the Last Chance Hotel.

'Professor Papperspook, welcome,' said Mr Bunn, bowing so low his nose almost touched the carpet and Seth could see his trousers straining at the back. 'We are honoured to have a guest of your immense reputation.'

A small girl emerged from behind the professor's voluminous skirts. She looked about nine and as if she'd arrived straight from school in a straight black skirt and cardigan and a stiff white blouse buttoned to her neck.

Professor Papperspook shooed the girl out and pushed her forwards. 'Gloria Troutbean, daughter of my oldest friend. I have always been proud of my connections to the great and glorious Troutbeans.' She gave a proud and wintry smile.

Gloria could almost be trying to be the negative of her colourful companion. Straight, jet-black hair fell evenly either side of her face, which was the colour of last week's milk. She didn't even nod in greeting, just glared down at the faded red swirls of the worn carpet, glancing up just once and blinking her peculiar, colourless eyes.

Darinder Dunster-Dunstable scampered towards the newcomers on his short little legs. He was only a head taller than Gloria. He gripped first hers, then Professor Papperspook's hand with his surprisingly wide and strong fingers, which reminded Seth of chicken drumsticks.

'Dunster-Dunstable – where have I heard your name?' asked the professor, rattling her fingers thoughtfully on her chin.

'Maybe you are more familiar with the Great Gandolfini? My stage name.' The short boy made a poor attempt to sound modest.

'The talented young illusionist? That's you? No? Amazing! I keep saying how I must take Gloria to see your show.'

Darinder gave a bow. 'Let me know a date. I'd be chuffed to bits if you'd let me get you the best seats in the house.'

Mr Bunn cleared his throat. 'Dear Professor, I expect you would welcome some refreshment after your journey.' He clicked his fingers at Seth, who was still trying to shoulder Darinder Dunster-Dunstable's heavy bags. 'And some help with your luggage.'

Mr Bunn disappeared through the door into the kitchen with a wave of his hands, leaving Seth to lead the way up the winding, uneven stairs, past a painting of a tiger and reaching a portrait of a woman in a madly fruited hat on the first-floor landing.

Dunster-Dunstable turned to Professor Papperspook while Seth fumbled with the keys to his room.

'Have you heard the news? Dr Thallomius is here. We will be showing our skills to the great man himself.'

His face puckered in excitement, but Professor Papperspook paled and her gaudy clothes appeared to shift then resettle.

'Dr Thallomius is here?' She folded her arms across her chest. 'Then I must tell him exactly what I think. Getting some of the very oldest and most noble families to go through this ridiculous procedure. Shameful.'

Seth puzzled over these words as he deposited Darinder's bags in his room. What 'procedure' was Professor Papperspook referring to? Something to do with 'showing their skills' to Dr Thallomius, whatever that meant.

But if Papperspook looked distressed about this, Dunster-Dunstable's grin only grew wider and he rubbed his hands. 'Sounds like this evening is going to be even more fun than I hoped.'

# 5. The Final Plump Raspberry

Back down in the kitchen after settling the new arrivals into their rooms, Seth whipped up a froth of cream for the pavlova, amazed to think the important guests would get to try something he'd made all by himself, even though he knew Tiffany would get all the credit. When he placed the final plump raspberry on the swirled meringue creation, Seth knew the dessert looked absolutely stunning.

'You colossal idiot,' came a voice from behind him.

He hated the way she always sneaked up on him.

'You've used raspberries, dimwit.'

'They are kind of an important part of a raspberry pavlova.'

'Not if this main guy, this Thallomius, is allergic to them. You brainless wonder. You actually are even worse than your good-for-nothing dad, aren't you? I said *strawberries*. I said a *strawberry* pavlova. Are you trying to make me look the world's biggest piece of stupid?'

Had Tiffany deliberately mixed him up? Seth knew she found nothing more fun than having him on the end of a hook, how she loved to see him dangle and squirm. But there was never any point in arguing with her. What was crucial was making sure their VIP guest would get a dessert he wasn't allergic to.

But Seth was also cross with himself. It was drummed into him to always know the guests' special requirements and he should have known his VIP guest was allergic to raspberries. He should have seen Tiffany's scheme coming and he fumed inwardly.

'It wouldn't be good to have a guest die on us, Seppi. Particularly if it looks like it's my fault,' yelled Tiffany in his ear. She made a sudden lunge and Seth feared she would grab his wonderful creation and smash it to the ground. Or worse, right in his face. He snatched the pavlova out of her reach and clasped it protectively, making the whipped cream wobble.

'Well at least *I* haven't spent years at a school for chefs without even knowing what a pavlova is,' Seth snapped back, the words out of his mouth before he could stop them.

Tiffany's eyes narrowed with anger and malice. Seth took a deep breath. He had never spoken back to her before.

There was a long moment while Seth tensed, felt the air charge and waited for the whiplash that was coming.

'I'll do something else for Dr Thallomius,' he stammered quickly, before she could even speak. 'Something just for him. Something really special,' he promised, carefully sliding the perfect pavlova inside the huge refrigerator and slamming the door before Tiffany could get her delicate, mean, milk-white hands on it.

'You'll do something outstanding,' said Tiffany.

The jangle of a bell made them both look up. There was a line of old-fashioned bells above the kitchen door that connected to each of the bedrooms. If they rang it meant someone wanted room service.

Room Six. Gregorian Kingfisher was requesting room service.

Seth nodded, eyes glued to that ringing bell, desperate to flee.

Tiffany watched the bell chime again as she lolled against the refrigerator giving a slow, wide, pink yawn.

Then her blue eyes snapped wide open.

'Hey. It could be your big chance, Seppi. Get your talent spotted. They might offer to take you away from all this. You'll be set on a road to fame and fortune.'

'No, Tiffany.' He paused in the doorway. 'Because you'll make sure you tell everyone you made it.'

She tilted her head to one side and gave a gloriously winning smile. 'Or this time I might tell them that it was really all you. All your work,' she crooned. 'What do you think?'

Seth looked into Tiffany's beautiful eyes and couldn't help feel a flash of hope.

Just for a second she had him believing her. Just for a second he thought she was dangling a chance. Then her face creased up and she barked out her hateful laugh.

'Oh, that is good! Believe that's going to happen, do you? Dream on Seppi. I know you are not completely awful at cooking.' She prodded at a gravy stain smeared on the apron over his blue tunic. 'But don't forget you are just a washer of saucepans. Always will be. You'll never leave this place. Every time I come home you will still be here in your rightful place, up to your elbows in potato peelings. You know you will. You'll never be like your dad.'

Seth felt his insides tightening into a fierce ball again. He backed away slowly and made a dash for the stairs, Tiffany's barking laughter echoing in his ears.

Only a brilliant recipe was going to keep Tiffany from tormenting him. And she would take all the credit. She always would. No wonder he could never see himself ever escaping from this place.

# 6. HERB TEA AND SHORTBREAD

As Seth reached the guest floor, Count Marred's face appeared from Dr Thallomius's room.

As his eyes locked with Seth's his face changed, the wrinkles in his face scrunching like paper.

'Um. Oh, we were wondering. Any chance of a cup of tea? And a jug of just hot water for me and my good friend Doctor Thallomius here – when you have a moment, no hurry at all.'

'Yes, of course,' said Seth.

Seth finally reached Gregorian Kingfisher's room

along the hall to answer the summons of the bell. He knocked twice and, getting no reply, stepped inside cautiously, wondering if he was too late. Then something immediately caught his attention.

On the desk opposite the door was a mirror with the same dark glass and dark wood as the one his father had left him. Seth crossed to the desk and picked it up, thinking the mirror was his.

The minute he held it in his hand, two things happened.

He could tell right away that the mirror felt quite different to his own, even though, as he caught the reflection of his pale face and worried eyes, he felt the same strange sensation as he did whenever he looked into his own mirror, as if he wanted to dive right into the glass.

And a voice behind him barked, 'What on earth are you doing?'

Seth turned clumsily, his elbow catching the corner of a mottled box made of a bumpy wood marked 'moustache care kit'. He only just stopped the neatly assembled combs and brushes tumbling on to the floor.

Seth also dropped the mirror.

Gregorian Kingfisher darted to catch it and so did Seth and they nearly crashed heads.

Seth felt his face turn crimson, garbling that he was room service.

'Are you indeed? Well, a bit late!' said Kingfisher acidly, looking at Seth as if he'd caught him stealing. 'I sorted myself out. Just get out.'

'Yes sir. Of course, sir.'

Apologizing once again, Seth fled back down to the kitchen, not forgetting he had to fetch tea for Room One, aware that the pile of washing-up was forming into an impossible tower and he still had to think of a new dessert for Doctor Thallomius.

He arrived, slightly breathless, at the door of Room One a few minutes later. 'Tea and hot water. And shortbread – lemon and cinnamon. I hope you like it crumbly.'

Seth crossed the room to the table where the man with the disfigured face was silhouetted in a chair, teasing out something from a small orange pouch. There was a herbal smell in the room and Seth smelt tea, green with a hint of grass.

Dr Thallomius approached him with tiny steps, a kindly look in his eye and an apology for Seth having to bring them something when he was so obviously busy.

Placing the tea tray down, Seth caught sight of a yellow sheet of paper and couldn't stop himself sneaking a little look:

*You are cordially invited to the*
*Last Chance Hotel to oversee a demonstration*
*by the following candidates who have applied to*
*go through the Prospect selection procedure.*

A list of names followed.

Dr Thallomius was at his side. 'Let me introduce my old friend Count Marred, my lad. What is your name?'

No guest in his whole life had ever been interested in his name before.

'Seth Seppi,' he managed to reply.

Dr Thallomius seized him by the hand as if delighted to meet him and Seth thought the old gentleman must have made a mistake. He didn't like to explain that he was only the kitchen boy.

The Count smiled widely. 'Who'd have thought my old friend Thallomius would be here,' he chuckled. 'Glad I decided to put myself through this infernal procedure the day you were in charge old fella. Should make things easier.'

'I am always completely fair,' twinkled Thallomius, shaking his head. 'Even to you.'

He reached to pat Count Marred on the shoulder and leant against the wall and Seth had the strangest sensation, almost as if the wall sighed as the old man touched it.

Dr Thallomius followed Seth to the door. 'Quite remote here isn't it? Do you have family, Seth?'

Seth found himself smiling. 'Just trees for ever, really. Guess my parents must have liked trees.'

'Liked? They're no longer around?'

'Not any more.' Seth felt the choke in his voice as he said it. He didn't know exactly how long it had been since he'd last seen his father. But it had been so long that Seth had given up hope of ever seeing him again.

'Sorry to hear that,' said Dr Thallomius, and he pressed something into Seth's hand.

Seth had discovered people didn't usually tip the kitchen boy – the boy who laid the tables and took out the rubbish and polished the candlesticks. If anyone left tips they were normally grabbed by Mr and Mrs Bunn.

But Dr Thallomius had given him a thick, heavy coin. Seth opened his mouth to protest, but Dr Thallomius closed Seth's hand over the gift.

'If I were you I'd put that somewhere safe. Now, off you go and get your work done. It's been an honour to meet you.'

Seth swallowed, convinced Dr Thallomius was

mixing him up with someone else. 'What is your favourite food, sir, I mean for a dessert, sir?' It was all he could think of to say, because he really wanted to thank this wonderful old gentleman somehow.

'Apricots,' said Dr Thallomius.

'Apricots,' nodded Seth, his mind quickly beginning to whir through possible recipes.

'Come on, Thallomius,' said Count Marred, in a gravelly voice. 'Let's have this tea, catch up on old news, then there's a game of four-handed brag being set up downstairs. I'd like to meet our fellow Prospect contenders. See who I'm up against. And if at all possible, I should like to win some money off them first.'

The mention of money made Seth feel for the coin in his pocket. It felt thick and heavy and when he took it out to look at it, his heart gave a start to see the glint of yellow like it was real gold. But why would Dr Thallomius give him a gold coin? Surely it had been a mistake, but then the old man had been very insistent.

All Seth knew was that no matter how little time he had left and how many candlesticks needed polishing, he would find the time to make a dessert to bring a smile to the face of this old gentleman.

# 7. GRINNING WOMAN IN THE MAD HAT

**B**ut first, finally, Seth was able to make it all the way to the top floor to feed his poor cat. He reached his room, relieved to rid himself of the incriminating stolen fish head, tossing it into Nightshade's bowl, which lay in the middle of the scrap of very worn carpet.

'Nightshade . . . Nightshade? You have no idea the trouble I got into getting that meal for you.'

He moved past the narrow wardrobe that tilted to one side like the Leaning Tower of Pisa and sank on to his narrow bed. Its mattress was even lumpier than Henri's mashed potatoes. His black cat was curled asleep in the middle of his bed, melting into the dark, scratchy blanket, almost invisible in the gloom.

He picked up his own mirror, which was still on the cardboard box he used as a bedside table. He saw his thin face looking back at him: wide eyes, untidy hair and pale skin above his bright blue tunic. Then his mirror did what it always did and his reflection was replaced, this time by a vision of the painting of the grinning woman in the mad hat from the first-floor landing. He put it down hurriedly.

Nightshade stirred, stretched out her front paws, clawed at the bed covers and arched her back with a baleful look at Seth, grumpy that he'd woken her. Then she fell on the fish head hungrily.

'Talking of trouble. Nightshade, I need a recipe rather desperately. That pavlova is the best thing I've ever done,' he sighed, taking out the gold coin and showing it to Nightshade. 'But I need something even better for Dr Thallomius.' Seth dragged a hand through his hair. 'I just don't seem to be able to come up with the perfect idea.'

Nightshade gently padded over to him as he shifted on the thin mattress, making the springs protest. She leapt on to his lap and started digging her needle-sharp claws into his leg as if he were a cushion.

'You watched Dad for years. What d'you think, Nightshade? Ever see him do anything brilliant with apricots? Got any bright ideas?'

He tipped her on to the floor and she started clawing at a small hole. She'd probably seen a spider.

'You know, you're really in trouble when you start asking your cat for help.'

Seth went across to one of the places in his room where the plaster near an ancient beam had started to crumble away. Here was a large hole that was great for hiding things. He reached in and took out a glass jar with a worn label that had once said *Gilbert's Extra-Strong Pickles*, into which Seth had saved every penny of his meagre tips over the years, and thoughtfully added the gold coin. Nightshade was still clawing.

'What is it, a mouse? Or a spider?' She adored spiders. Sometimes he'd catch her looking gruesome with a couple of legs dangling out of her mouth.

She wasn't stopping. In fact, she was scrabbling and clawing a sizeable hole in the wall. Plaster was flying everywhere.

'Nightshade, stop! Last thing I need is a load of mess to clear up.'

She was covering herself in plaster.

Despite the mess and the hole in the wall Seth couldn't help laughing. 'You don't look black any more, you look grey. I'm going to have to change your name to Smoke.'

But when he bent down to examine the mess, he wasn't laughing any more. Then Nightshade started to paw at the hole again. 'No, Nightshade. Enough!'

He moved her roughly away, but she twisted from him and again stuck her paw deep in the hole and started clawing.

'What is it? You're not after a mouse or a spider, are you?'

Seth bent down and peered into the hole. There was something there. Seth reached in, feeling gently with the ends of his fingers, hoping it truly wasn't a mouse or a spider. He drew out what was hidden inside.

He could see right away it was a book, a small black book, well-used and so ancient he was afraid it might fall apart in his hands. As Seth lifted it, he could see its black cover had no markings, no lettering at all. But although it was old, someone had treasured it enough to bind it together by a thick scarlet thread.

He was so stunned to suddenly find something so

unusual, so old, and possibly very valuable in his drab and familiar room that before he'd even thought about it he found his fingers had unlaced the thread and opened the book.

# 8. THE STRANGE BLACK BOOK

The book felt warm, as if it was giving off a glow, and it seemed almost to settle and mould itself to his touch like it belonged there.

He perched on the end of his narrow bed, holding the book in his lap, and soon he was lost in thick pages full of jottings, doodles, pictures and angry crossing-outs.

Seth was thrilled to see that the book was mostly full of recipes, unusual recipes. A recipe for quince posset... one for roast pigeon... swan with chestnut stuffing. If there was one thing Seth loved, it was new recipes. And he had never seen recipes like these before.

The book was impossible to resist. Page after page of hints for making your own shoe polish and oven cleaner alongside a recipe for Dundee cake or a drink crammed with lots of different herbs and berries marked 'works well on dogs'.

Seth carried on leafing through the pages, desperately hoping to find something he could make for Dr Thallomius. He paused to peer at a sketch of a birdcage, very similar to the tiny birdcage that hung from the ceiling in the room where Mr Bunn secretly skulked with the newspaper most of the day. Only this birdcage seemed to be on fire and beneath it was written, 'firefly cage'.

Nightshade slipped smoothly on to the bed beside him and Seth reached out to stroke her fur. She still looked unlike her usual self, not being sootily black, but her green eyes stood out, looking at him with the wisdom of twin moons.

'It's like a gathering together of all sorts of home-made ideas for making stuff. Weird stuff some of it.' He was staring at a description of a small mirror, named a 'ruhnglas – for if your way is secret'. That was no good.

'It's not just recipes, Nightshade. Someone must have liked collecting and experimenting. A bit like me. But what I really need is something new and delicious with apricots. There was a section here somewhere called family favourites.'

He flicked the pages back again and there it was. 'Apricot Delice'. Seth scanned the recipe. Simple, yet delicate. Perfect. Seth closed the book and breathed a sigh of relief. For once, it almost seemed as if things were on his side, almost as if time had even slowed for him.

'Right, Nightshade! I need you. We have to be quick. We are on the hunt for apricots.'

He turned to where Nightshade was busy cleaning the light covering of dust with her paws. She stopped and her low silhouette slunk behind him without hesitation, moving as fluidly as a liquid shadow as Seth headed down the stairs and out into the hotel's garden on his quest for apricots. The daylight was already disappearing fast. Time was running out.

# 9. AN ACCUSING FINGER

Seth slipped back in through the lobby, his tunic pockets bulging with apricots, listening out anxiously to see if he had been missed. But as he passed the hotel lounge, he was relieved to hear Horatio Bunn being jolly and offering drinks. Count Marred had said something about a game of cards and it sounded like they were all getting to know each other.

That meant no ringing bells. Even so, that dessert was literally going to have to be the work of a moment.

First, Seth laid the long gleaming table in the dining room, under a painting of two men sharing a meal of bread and cheese. He was almost out of time and just hoped no one would notice he hadn't polished the candlesticks.

Eight chairs waited in anticipation. The great ornate carved chair at the head of the table was where Dr Thallomius would sit.

Seth set up heated trays so the food would be kept warm in the centre of the table, as no one was allowed in to serve the guests. The meal was to be eaten in private, with only the guests present, behind closed doors.

Mr Bunn had drilled into his staff every small detail of what was requested for this secret feast. Except telling anyone what the occasion was. Seth could not help but wonder about it as he moved a small table to just behind Dr Thallomius's chair that would be perfect for the apricot dessert, picturing the exact glass dish he would serve it in.

He had caught that tiny glimpse of the paper in Dr Thallomius's room. Something about being invited for a demonstration, candidates for some-thing called 'the Prospect selection procedure'. What on earth was that? And why did everyone react so strongly to hearing Dr Thallomius was here? Who exactly *was* their VIP guest? Seth was just about to head back to the kitchen when he stopped and counted the places again.

Dr Thallomius, Professor Papperspook, Gloria Troutbean, Darinder Dunster-Dunstable, Angelique Squerr, Gregorian Kingfisher, Count Marred.

There were only seven guests. So why had he been told to lay the table for eight?

Laughter drifted from the lounge, along with the chiming of the grandfather clock's musical striking of the hour, which reminded Seth it would soon be time to bring in the food from the kitchen. And he still had a dessert to do.

Seth passed the lounge again and peeked in to where Dr Thallomius, Count Marred, Professor Papperspook and Darinder Dunster-Dunstable were squashed in around a low table in comfy chairs, playing cards, next to the fire Seth had laid earlier, which cast a lively flickering glow on their laughing faces. Others were having drinks at the shiny chrome cocktail bar.

The lounge was the cosiest room in the hotel. No heavy wood panelling here, it was painted in a pale colour that reflected the light, with a modest fireplace in white marble. Even the paintings were cheerfully framed scenes of people partying and diving into swimming pools.

Marred made a joke and everyone burst into peals of laughter. Good, everyone was occupied.

When Seth arrived back at the kitchen, Henri greeted him angrily and pointed to the teetering pile of washing up, but Seth walked straight past him and told him he would do it after the dinner.

He took a deep breath and propped up the mysterious black book in front of him on the counter. He followed the instructions exactly, separating eggs then whisking the yolks, frothing them to a thick creaminess with a little lemon zest, then adding the flesh from the apricots, a sprinkle of cinnamon and carefully dribbling in just the right amount of Marsala wine. In just three minutes he spooned his dessert into an elegant stemmed dish. It was light and fluffy, smooth and a buttery yellow like custard.

He closed his eyes and hoped, as he took a nervous taste.

It was as utterly perfect and as delicious as he had hoped. Seth felt a fluttering that told him with certainty that today was his day.

'Is this it?' Tiffany was by his side, jolting him back to the present.

She bestowed one of her most winning smiles that replaced just the vaguest hint of an anxious look that had crossed her face. 'For a moment I thought you were going to let me down, pot washer. And I really wouldn't be in your shoes if you ever risked anything so stupid.'

Seth carried the dessert carefully though the kitchen. He had added a finishing touch of slices of plump, fresh apricot and placed the whole perfect confection ready in a bowl of ice to keep it at the correct temperature. He checked that the label, which read *For the special delight of Dr Thallomius*, was in place and held his creation out to Tiffany as they arrived at the lobby, where Mr and Mrs Bunn were hovering anxiously.

Kingfisher, Dr Thallomius and Count Marred were outside the dining room and Professor Papper-spook, Gloria Troutbean, Angelique Squerr and Dunster-Dunstable were watching from the stairs, waiting for the announcement that the food for the feast was ready.

All eyes were on the exquisite dessert in Seth's hands as he tried to carefully hand it to Tiffany. Tiffany turned and gave one of her sugary simpers.

'Oh Seth,' she said, in a pathetic voice, 'as I slaved so hard on the dessert, perhaps you can do a little work and wouldn't mind placing it on the table.'

He felt eyes boring into him as he walked into the

dining room, past where Kingfisher was impatiently holding open the carved wooden door to where the rest of the feast lay ready.

'It seems that the feast will be starting a few minutes later than the appointed hour of six-thirty.' Kingfisher snapped as Seth flew past him. 'The ritual is aimed at being both fair and understanding and allows for these sorts of blunders,' continued Kingfisher, throwing Seth a withering glance that said in no uncertain terms that Seth had unwittingly managed to annoy the young man again.

Kingfisher checked his watch in an impatient manner. 'So take this as your official five-minute warning of the start of the feast. The door will now be locked, as part of strict procedures to prevent any last-minute tinkering or sabotage. The feast is held in secrecy, away from prying eyes. We know you would never want outsiders bustling in and out of the room,' he said as Seth scuttled back out of the room, just as Kingfisher started to close the door.

'We understand that some of you may be bringing precious and secretive devices to the feast and would want to keep them away from the prying eyes of outsiders,' he said smoothly. 'So, candidates, now is the time. Go and fetch anything you need for your demonstrations. Please return here in exactly five minutes with anything you need. Then the doors will be unlocked. Do not be late.'

The heavy door was slammed shut and Mr Bunn and Kingfisher locked the door with the two keys – one at the top, one at the bottom – and all the guests began a rush upstairs.

Seth hadn't a clue what precious and secretive devices Kingfisher could possibly be referring to, or what anyone would be demonstrating. He didn't understand why the whole meal was cloaked in secrecy or why it needed such fancy procedures. He was fascinated by it all. But at that moment, none of that mattered. He knew that the dessert was beautiful and perfect and he felt this was definitely the day his life was going to change.

# 10. IT WAS ALL SETH

Seth couldn't help but return in five minutes to watch as Mr Bunn and Kingfisher unsealed the room. First, Angelique Squerr and Dr Thallomius took their seats on the far side of the table and then there was a flurry of excited chatter as Professor Papperspook guided in Gloria, followed by a clearly excited Dunster-Dunstable rubbing his hands, with Count Marred and Kingfisher bringing up the rear.

Seven guests. Seth looked around eagerly to see who the eighth might be, but he suddenly felt a heavy hand on his collar and smelt Henri's garlicky breath as he was hauled towards the kitchen to face the pile of washing up that had grown to such a tower it was almost waving at him.

Seth rolled up his sleeves and started to run foamy water, unable to suppress his curiosity about what was happening behind that closed door.

If kindly Dr Thallomius was seriously impressed by the dessert, might Seth have someone he could confess his dreams to? Someone he could maybe ask for help in getting away and finding somewhere he could practise his cooking and not to have to do it in secret?

But his insides seemed to sink under the weight of knowing that he would first have to stand up to Tiffany if he was going to announce that both the pavlova and the apricot delice were his creations. Would anyone believe him?

As he prepared for battle with the crusted saucepans and overflowing bins, Tiffany's words came back in a rush to haunt him.

*'You'll never leave this place. Every time I come home you will still be here in your rightful place, up to your elbows in potato peelings. You know you will. You will never be like your dad.'*

He rolled up his sleeves and moved towards the

terrifying pile. He lifted the first saucepan into the soapy water.

His real life was about a million miles from his dreams. How would he ever become a great chef like his father? It was never going to happen. He was never going to be able to prove to Tiffany – to everyone – that he wasn't simply fit for washing-up.

He picked up the first plate and dunked it in the water. Then he stopped, bent his head and groaned with a deep weariness.

'The only way it's going to happen is if I make it happen,' he said. He was talking to himself. The kitchen was completely deserted, not even Nightshade was around. No one was checking on what he was doing.

He slipped the black book out from where he had tucked it inside his tunic and found this time it was so warm his hands dried the instant he touched it.

'My only way out of here is if I practise and practise and become as good a chef as my father, not if I spend my time washing up!' He flicked through the pages of the black book, the most exciting and enticing book of recipes ever.

Seth felt that stirring thrill of excitement in his chest. There really were the most incredible ideas in there.

Swan with chestnut stuffing. Well he wasn't going to rustle that up in a hurry.

But there was one here that he could try. And it would take his mind off what was happening behind that closed door. How long would it take them to eat the main course and get to dessert? Seth checked the clock again. He had at least an hour to fill and he'd only be nervously twitching – cooking would take his mind of things.

And that washing up would still be there in the morning.

He propped the book up in front of him and began to cook.

## 11. Something He Ate

The guests had been cocooned in the dining room for two hours now and Seth decided to tiptoe into the cramped writing room next door and put his ear to the wall to see if he could find out anything. But before he could even start to listen, there was a terrific crash. Seth stepped back from the wall in alarm. What had happened? It sounded like a chair falling over.

He heard the door to the dining room burst open. As he dashed into the lobby, he saw that Mr Bunn had got there first and was flapping about in a daze, looking around wildly, waving his hands in panic.

'Help!' he cried. 'HELP!' he added more loudly, tearing at his hair and staring around.

Seth peeped around the door frame into the dining room, unsure what to do. What on earth was happening?

Everyone was on their feet crowding around something.

Norrie Bunn, Henri and Tiffany all rushed past Seth. Pointy-eared Darinder Dunster-Dunstable was waving something around. It was the long-stemmed dish that had contained the apricot dessert.

Then the group parted and Seth could see that everyone was crowding around the small figure of Dr Thallomius, who was clutching his hands to his throat. His face was turning purple, he was staggering and fighting for breath.

Professor Papperspook rushed forward and slapped him vigorously on the back, there was a terrible cry from someone, Seth thought it was Count Marred, as Dr Thallomius flailed at the air and collapsed into a heap on the carpet.

There were confused cries of 'Is he choking?' 'It's something he ate!' and, 'There must be something we can do!'

Seconds later, Papperspook shook her head gravely from where she was kneeling beside Dr Thallomius. 'It is too late for help. I'm afraid there is nothing to be done.'

'No!' wailed Count Marred. 'It cannot be!'

'I'm sorry, but Dr Thallomius is dead,' announced Papperspook. 'And it looks like poison.'

A small series of gasps went around the room, sounding like a whisper.

Seth felt as if his insides had been hollowed out.

Kingfisher spoke loudly, saying that he was in charge, but it was lost in the clamour of hysterical voices.

'Gloria, look away my dear. Let's get you away from here.' Professor Papperspook grabbed Gloria and started to hustle her from the room, trying to shield her eyes. 'I don't want you to have to see this.'

Dunster-Dunstable waved the long-stemmed glass dish in the air, almost swiping Angelique across the nose. 'The dessert,' he cried. 'He ate this and he died. The dessert killed him.'

'That was very clearly labelled to be eaten only by Dr Thallomius,' trilled Professor Papperspook, her parting shot as she and Gloria fled up the spiral stairs.

Seth was frozen to the spot. He was aware of Mr

Bunn and Tiffany sharing a shocked glance. Then Dunster-Dunstable advanced on Tiffany. She took a step back. The boy was much smaller than her, but still Tiffany hunched back alarmed as he moved closer, waving the dessert glass in her face.

Somehow everyone seemed to move at the same time and Seth could see Dr Thallomius, completely motionless in a heap, his hand still gripping a long silver spoon, his eyes wide, his mouth open. Seth wanted to turn away, but his eyes seemed locked to the horrible scene.

The confusion and clamour was drowned out by the real horror before him and for a moment all he could hear was the pounding of blood in his ears and that nightmare vision of Dr Thallomius's dead body on the floor. His nose picked up a faint scent, like bitter almonds. *Strange.*

'I'll handle this,' said a voice. Seth thought it was Kingfisher, again trying to get some control. 'We were told this was your work, Tiffany Bunn. That dessert! What did you put in it?' he snapped.

Tiffany stared around, her eyes wide in horror, and she started to shrink back into the corner. Her father threw a protective arm around her shoulder.

Count Marred clasped his head in his hands and let out a huge, rending wail. 'My friend. My friend is dead.' He shook his large head from side to side. He began to advance on Tiffany, who was now cowering in the farthest corner. 'Why did you do this?'

Tiffany's face drained of colour as she shrank against the wall, her eyes big and wary.

Then she seemed to regain her confidence, and shrugged off her father. 'It was nothing to do with me!' she announced, as she stood up straight and her gaze began combing the room. She stopped as her eyes locked with Seth's where he hovered just outside the dining room door, frozen, still unable to truly take in what had happened.

Then her face grew fierce and she moved forward in a swift movement, shoving aside Angelique, then Dunster-Dunstable, who was still waving his glass aloft. She moved relentlessly forwards.

Everyone stepped out of her way as she advanced.

Seth felt her grab him by the collar and he was shoved, stumbling, in front of the crowd.

He faced many pairs of shocked and accusing eyes. Tiffany held the back of his tunic in a powerful grip. There was no escape. Nowhere to hide.

'The desserts were nothing to do with me at all,' she announced. 'It was all Seth. He's the one responsible.'

A murmur raced around the room and started to grow.

'Don't look at me. It wasn't me. If anyone here poisoned someone it was Seth!' Tiffany declared, her voice ringing with confidence.

Seth saw Kingfisher approach, his face livid.

Before he even knew what was happening, Seth felt himself bundled out of the dining room and was shoved from behind towards the broom cupboard. He catapulted into the darkness and the door was locked.

PART TWO

## 12. A Search for Deadly Poison

Seth groped in the cramped, dark space, his only company a well-worn mop, a bucket and a box of rusty tools. He turned the bucket over to use as a stool and slumped down, drawing his hands through his untidy hair. It was difficult to take in what had just happened. Impossible to believe that kindly Dr Thallomius was really dead.

And it looked like everyone thought it was something to do with that apricot dessert he had made. But how could it be? He sank back shakily.

Only a few hours ago he'd been convinced today was his day, his chance to turn the tables on Tiffany and change his life. Instead, Henri's portentous prediction when he'd seen that firefly had come horribly true. Murder had come to the Last Chance Hotel.

'So,' hissed a voice from the other side of the locked door. 'Plan A, I guess you sit there and just keep your fingers crossed things will sort themselves out and maybe they'll realize you are completely innocent.'

Seth moved closer to the door. Had someone come to let him out? And just who was it speaking in that low, purring voice?

'That security chap has called all of them into the hotel lounge to make their statements. That means now's your best chance to search everyone's rooms.' A female voice. It was a strange accent, soft. 'You need to find out who is really responsible or you'll get the blame. Be brave, Seth. Get to it.'

Seth felt small and terrified and not at all brave. 'I'll get caught and things will be even worse.'

'They won't sit in that room for ever, looking at each other like they don't trust each other a whisker. You have to do it now.'

Still Seth didn't move.

'Not the first time you've been locked in with the mops and the buckets is it? You've dreamt of getting away the last couple of years. Prison might not be so bad. Thought you'd at least miss the garden. So, it's goodbye then,' went on the voice, more urgent now. 'Or . . . you could remember the toolbox . . .'

How did the voice know Seth had been locked in this cupboard many times?

Seth sat for just one moment longer, then he scrabbled around. The toolbox was where it always was and in the darkness he groped for a screwdriver and removed the hinges from the door. They came away easily.

'Who are you?' Seth asked, looking around as he emerged into the softly twinkling lights of the deserted lobby.

He felt something move past his legs, but it was only Nightshade, who leapt on a carved figure, one that Henri spent his free time whittling.

'I hate these things,' the voice hissed as Night-shade pawed at it.

Seth stared at the cat. 'Nightshade . . . that's not *you* speaking?'

'Looks that way. But don't go asking me to explain.'

'Hang on a minute. I mean . . .' He shook his head hard. This could not be real.

'I'll tell you the truth, Seth,' she purred. 'I've always thought I could talk, I just never saw a reason to do so until you needed my help.' Nightshade darted ahead of him up the stairs. 'You are in a pretty pickle and we need to move. Master key, Seth!'

'What are we doing, Nightshade?'

'My whiskers, do I have to tell you, Seth? Someone brought poison to this hotel. Let's try to find it before they have a chance to get rid of it.'

On any other day, he would have at least paused to puzzle out how it had happened that his cat had started talking, but he was already too stunned by everything else happening, his thoughts too busy imagining a hand seizing his shoulder and an angry voice demanding why he was no longer safely locked up. If he really was going to sneak out and try to search some of the rooms for poison, he had to do it fast.

His terrified legs managed to move and he sneaked past the hotel lounge where, behind the closed door, he could hear agitated, raised voices. He dived to swiftly take the big key from under the counter of the welcome desk and followed Nightshade as she padded up the stairs, his breath coming short and fast, fearful of being caught at any moment.

'But how will I even know what the poison is?' Seth asked helplessly.

'You think. You were in the dining room. I bet you smelt the poison. Use your nose.'

Seth forced himself to think of the dining room. He had to focus on his nose and not think of the horror of watching Dr Thallomius writhing in agony. Yes, there had been a smell.

'There was something. A sort of sweetly bitter smell. Like bitter almonds.'

Had that been the poison? It must have been, because he'd never come across that smell in the hotel before. Nightshade was standing by the first door and he unlocked it, still not quite believing that he was taking advice from his cat.

'Professor Papperspook's room.' Nightshade slid past his legs. 'Looked right upset when that Darinder mentioned Dr Thallomius was here. Let's see what she's hiding.'

Seth went straight over to a smart black leather case with heavy straps. It was sitting on the desk, wide open. And it contained bottles. Seth couldn't believe his luck – two rows of small, intricate glass bottles, eight in total. Perfect for bringing poison to the hotel.

Each had a label. *Lark Song, Blackbird Warning,*

*Robin Calling* and *Blue Tit Cry*. What did they mean? Gingerly, Seth put his nose close to the bottles. But he could smell nothing.

'I'm going to have to take out a stopper.'

'Just be quick.' Nightshade was right behind him.

He seized a bottle and pulled out the stopper. Instantly, the room was filled with the sudden powerful swell of birdsong, as loud as if he'd set off an alarm in the room. As if a flock of birds was right there with him. He thrust the stopper back in and the sound immediately ceased. Seth breathed again, darting a look over his shoulder and waiting to see if the noise had brought a footfall on the stair.

'Can't you be bit quieter, Seth?'

They were both still for a moment. Seth was convinced he heard a creak from below and his heart lurched.

'Perhaps I'll just go and . . .' said Nightshade, slipping out of the door, returning a moment later saying the coast was clear and everyone was still in the lounge.

'But do get on with it. Sure you used to move a lot faster,' she growled.

'Terrific. I've got a cat that's decided to tell me she learnt to speak ages ago and she just insults me.'

But Seth followed, his heart pounding, his eyes

shifting left and right as he crept next door into Gloria Troutbean's room, where he searched under the stern eye of a portrait of a woman with a long face who looked like she'd love to squeal and give him away.

Nightshade sat on the bed and began to slowly lick her front paw.

'Nightshade,' he said irritably, 'Please can you not sit on the bed. You know you're not allowed anywhere near the guest rooms. If Norrie finds so much as a single cat hair I'll be dead anyway.'

The cat instantly leapt off the bed.

'Tell you what, Seth, I'll keep a look out.' She slipped out again and Seth examined some very weird-looking boots, a strange design with extra-thick soles. He picked them up and turned them over.

'Who *are* these people?' he muttered. 'Do they all have weird stuff?'

He was crouched low and his nose told him that somewhere in this room there was the smell of something . . . pears maybe, but unusual.

He followed his nose, which took him to the bed. He fumbled around under the mattress and pillow, reached in and he was right, there was something hidden there. He brought out a paper bag, which he opened hopefully.

And he was staring at pear drops. A lot of pear drops.

His hopes sagged.

A creak came from outside and there was a soft warning pawing on the door. Seth held his breath and kept his ear pricked.

If the questioning in the hotel lounge was over, any moment now someone was going to realize he was no longer under lock and key. He had to get back downstairs.

'I should never have listened to you, Nightshade,' he muttered.

All he could do was stay silent and hope Miss Troutbean was not coming.

Then the soft pawing came again and he hoped this was Nightshade giving him the all-clear signal because he slipped straight outside.

Nightshade led the flight back down the stairs, but stopped halfway, Seth almost tumbled over her. He realized why she'd stopped. There was someone in the lobby below.

He waited, breathing heavily, his shoulder next to a portrait of a tiger that looked like it would love to reach out a claw and take his left ear off. He positioned himself ready to fly downstairs the moment the coast was clear and get back into that cupboard the second he got the chance, or fling himself back up the stairs if he was spotted.

Voices. And they were coming from right outside the cupboard where he was supposed to be imprisoned. Any second now someone would open it and discover that Seth wasn't inside.

Seth's heart hammered painfully. He should never have done it. It had been stupid to go upstairs. Now there was no way he'd slip back inside without anyone knowing he'd escaped.

This was what happened when you found yourself taking advice from a talking cat.

He was doomed.

# 13. ENTRANCE OF FILM-STAR HAIR

'See sense, Kingfisher – I can't believe you're being so obstinate,' said a girl's voice, rising.

'I am in charge of security here, Angelique,' replied the voice of Kingfisher, who was pacing the lobby below. He shook his shoulders and straightened his suit. 'Please remember.'

But after a short pause, in a voice that told Seth she was used to organizing other people, Angelique Squerr added, 'But you are following basic procedure? All exits and communication channels are sealed?'

Kingfisher snapped. 'What's the point? I took statements from everyone. They all ate the same food. Except that dessert. It's an open and shut case.' Seth heard the sound of papers being shuffled. '*He produced a dessert secretly in a small cubbyhole behind the deep freeze so that no one could see what he was doing.*' It sounded as if Kingfisher was reading aloud from notes. '*He did it last minute and then the dessert was labelled very clearly for Dr Thallomius. It was placed directly behind him, so that there was no risk of anyone else eating it. The very second the dessert arrived, the door was locked.*'

Seth listened with a creeping feeling of horror.

It was all true. That was exactly how it had happened.

The dessert had been the last thing to go into the dining room – and after that the door was locked. And from the moment it was unlocked, the dining room had been full of people. So, when had it been poisoned?

Surely no one would have taken a great risk of slipping something into Dr Thallomius's dessert in a room full of people? And, if so, how had they managed it without being spotted?

That seemed extraordinarily unlikely, so how else could the poison have got into that dessert glass?

'Murder by the kitchen boy is the only thing that adds up,' said Kingfisher smoothly. 'Unless someone was utterly brazen and slipped something in that dish in full view of everyone? And managed to do it without anyone noticing what they were up to? I mean, come on. Really how else could the poison possibly have got into that dessert? You answer me that and I'll arrest them instead.'

Even when he'd been accused and locked in the cupboard, Seth had clung to a hope that everyone would have to recognize he wasn't responsible for what had happened to Dr Thallomius. But the full chill of what they were saying was sinking in.

No one else could have done it.

How on earth had the poison really got into that dessert glass?

Unless he could find an answer for that, Seth had a terrifying vision of himself on a long uncomfortable ride in a police car before the evening was even over. Followed by a life in jail. What on earth was he going to do?

'All right, so it appears clear-cut,' said Angelique, although her voice was full of curiosity and doubt. 'And as I was sitting in front of that dessert the whole evening and no one went near that table, I can tell you that is not the answer either. What we have here is a real mystery. And do think about who we are dealing with here.'

Seth was puzzling and worrying so frantically, he thought he must have misheard what she said next.

'The Sorcerer General has been murdered. Just imagine Gregorian, just for one moment, that you are wrong. And that you just let all the other suspects go.'

*Sorcerer*? Seth's brain reeled again. What was she talking about?

'I had that Seppi character fixed as a bad lot from the start. I can get him to confess,' Kingfisher continued, his voice like cold steel. 'I can get it wrapped up and we can all be out of here tonight.'

There was the soft rustling of silk and Angelique Squerr moved into view. She was wearing a black evening dress with a red cape and leant on a long, silver-topped, red-lacquered cane, which she lifted to point at Kingfisher's chest.

'Follow procedure. Get MagiCon here now. You know you must.'

Seth kept perfectly still, his ears pricked, Nightshade at his side, desperate to find out more.

'Don't interfere,' drawled Kingfisher.

Angelique tossed back her hair and jabbed at Kingfisher with the end of her cane. 'The most important sorcerer in the land has been murdered. You're really going to take on the whole investigation single-handed, Gregorian?'

Kingfisher's fingers worried at his moustache. 'If MagiCon rage on at me for wasting their time I shall blame you, Angelique. I'm telling you, this case could not be simpler.'

Heavy footsteps took Seth by surprise. Kingfisher was on the move. Seth flattened himself again against the central wall around which the stairs spiralled.

'And I should make sure you have thorough background on everyone before you close down communications because they will ask you,' Angelique called. 'Follow procedure!'

Seth listened hard, not yet daring to breathe normally, waiting for the second set of footsteps to follow, his heart beating rapidly as he waited. All he needed was one small chance to get back in that cupboard.

But there was no further sound of footsteps, all he could hear was Angelique's dress rustling. But what was she doing? She had drifted out of view. And as Seth listened, he thought he heard a crackle like static electricity.

He dared to move a little further down the stairs.

She was standing right next to Seth's favourite painting, a colour drawing of an owl, so lifelike Seth could imagine it coming alive and flying at night. She was feeling around the frame, her long, deft fingers going methodically around the edges.

Then she took a step back and lifted the cane above her head. Seth thought she was going to launch it into the picture.

He moved, his first instinct to protect the painting, but there was no time to grab the cane from her. He could only watch as the end of the cane crackled and a fierce jet of blue light that was as bright as Seth's tunic shot out. Sapphire sparkles crept and hovered around the edges of the picture before seeming to melt away.

Seth stood on the bottom stair, breathing so hard. What had just happened?

Angelique Squerr said without turning, 'All right, boy. Kingfisher's gone. And if you've been watching me and think you might have seen something – my very strong advice would be to forget it. Unless you want me joining those saying you should be taken away in handcuffs.'

## 14. A Connection

Seth swallowed and stepped down into the lobby. 'No, no, I haven't been watching you. And I didn't kill Dr Thallomius,' he added hurriedly. 'If you can help me at all, I'd really appreciate it.'

She was writing in a small notebook covered in shiny red leather.

Despite the glamour, the make-up and painted nails, one of the first things that struck Seth was that he reckoned she couldn't be much older than him.

Calling him *boy* was a bit much.

'I need to quickly look around. They'll be safe in that hotel lounge for about ten minutes. And I have questions you might be able to help with.'

There was something about the way she said it that made Seth ask: 'You've locked them in?' He turned, expecting to hear shouts and hammering on the door. But all he saw was Nightshade slipping away.

'No, I thought that might annoy them.' Angelique's nose wrinkled. 'So I placed a confusion enchantment on the door. If they touch it they forget why they wanted to leave in the first place.'

'Err,' Seth gulped, feeling utterly bewildered. 'I think a confusion enchantment on the door is ... fine.'

He watched, fascinated, as she ran her hands along the frame of a picture of a couple of horses who looked like they'd rather be somewhere else.

'You called Dr Thallomius the Sorcerer General. When you say "sorcerer" – what do you mean exactly?' he asked hesitantly.

'Head of our governing body, the Elysee, yes, he runs the magical community – ran.' She gulped and her face crumpled, just for a moment. Then she tossed her hair. 'At one time, he was best known for his magical inventions, but he closed his workshop years ago and devoted his life to service of magical people. That's the kind of man he was – he put the magical community first, always. Campaigned for magic to be a force for good.'

Seth thought of the short, kindly gentleman with the white hair, a round tummy and twinkle in his eye. He hadn't looked in the least like a VIP guest, let alone the head of the magical community. He'd looked like everyone's favourite grandfather.

'And when you say magical community?'

She threw him a mistrustful look. 'I know the magical world isn't what it used to be, but you are seriously telling me you've never even heard of the Elysee?'

'Erm,' muttered Seth. 'I've lived here my whole life.' He finished with a shrug. 'It's kind of quiet out here. I haven't heard of a lot of things.'

He only just managed not to blurt out he'd always thought magic existed only in those fairy tales with witches and poisoned apples and elves helping shoemakers at night.

She pointed with her cane, indicating that she expected him to accompany her up the narrow, twisted stairs. She marched ahead of him, stopping briefly to examine the picture of the tiger.

He followed, reminding himself he had to focus

on one important thing here – convincing everyone he had not killed Dr Thallomius. Could Angelique help him? Should he even trust her? What was she doing with that cane? She leant on it as she walked, but he wasn't convinced that was the reason she carried it.

'Has it really been so long since magical people were common?' she sighed as they reached the guest-floor landing. 'Healers, people you turned to in times of trouble. At one time, everyone knew magic as a force for good. Happy magic.' She shook her long hair. 'Now, what can you tell me about this place? How long have you lived here?'

'All my life.'

'Then you know this place better than anyone. You probably have all the answers.' She smiled at him expectantly.

Seth didn't think he had any answers. He certainly had plenty of questions.

'The Bunns are your parents?' she went on as she peered behind an ugly vase.

'No! My mother died when I was very young and my father worked here as a chef.'

'*Worked* here? Where is he now?'

'What is MagiCon?' Seth asked, quickly putting a question of his own.

'MagiCon – the Magical Constabulary . . . well, who do you think investigates crime in the magical community?'

'Why was Mr Kingfisher so reluctant to call them?'

'People do describe them as terrifying.' She lifted her cane high and tapped it gently against one of the walls. 'I suppose it might be intimidating being interrogated by magical people.'

'Terrifying? And they're coming here?' Seth squeaked, wondering just what a terrifying magical interrogation would be like and realizing he was probably soon going to find out. 'I really didn't do it.'

'I'd try not to worry.'

Not worry? Seth was quickly adjusting to the news that there really was such thing as magic in the world, which was astonishing enough. And adjusting to the fact that he was accused of murdering the chief sorcerer in the land. And now he was about to undergo a magical interrogation – could anything possibly get worse?

She turned and looked straight at him with eyes the colour of caramel, then lifted her cane again. This time, she rapped it against the wall hard.

Before Seth could even begin to ask what she was doing, he was startled to hear a growl from the wall as if in answer. It started low, like oncoming thunder, then first one wall, then all the walls on the landing began to gently shake. The rumbling and vibration grew until plaster started crumbling on to Seth's shoulders and he stared around him, fearful the hotel might start to collapse around their ears.

# 15. Two Problems

There was a loud snap like a lightning strike, then a low rumbling that sounded like a voice and just as Seth thought they should run, it all stopped.

'What on earth was that?' asked Seth, brushing plaster dust from his shoulders.

Angelique merely wrinkled her nose. 'The walls are trying to tell us something. Ever heard that before?'

'A really scary rumbling like the walls are speaking? Definitely not. I would have remembered.'

Seth's brain was buzzing as he followed her. He was thinking of the moment earlier that afternoon when Dr Thallomius had touched the wall. There had been a noise then, hadn't there, like the wall sighing? What did it mean?

'You said the murdered man – Dr Thallomius – was once a magical inventor. Err . . . what exactly is a magical invention?'

'Do you always have so many questions?' She threw him a scornful look and tossed her hair impatiently. 'You might have a teleport, that's magic so people can travel easily. Or a teleglobe – a magical way of communicating.' She looked at him as if trying to work out if he was too stupid to understand. 'Most sorcerers just use the usual ways of doing magic.' She turned and must have seen his blank look because the hair was tossed again. 'You know, like coming up with a charm, or you might create a potion to make people do things they didn't necessarily set out to do.'

Something made him think of that black book. That had been full of all sorts of things, not simply recipes, but weird scribblings, pictures and ideas he hadn't understood. Strange things, the like of which he had never seen before. Like that page with the picture of a tiny cage flowing with light.

'Would a magical invention be like a . . . a . . .' He began to stutter as he put together his thoughts. '. . . a firefly cage or a—'

He never got the chance to finish.

Angelique had swung around and was advancing on Seth, her short red cape flying. She flicked up the end of her cane and pointed it to press on his neck like a dagger.

'You spin me stories that you've never even heard of the magical community and then you come out with that!' she snapped, her arm raised high, the cane pressing in harder.

The only movement Seth could manage was to swivel his eyes to stay focused on the end of that cane. He would have swallowed, but didn't dare.

'What do you know about a firefly cage?' Angelique's eyes were blazing.

'I . . . I . . .' All he was aware of was that cane pressing in. 'I . . . I think I overheard one of the guests. I don't even know what it is.' He closed his eyes.

'A firefly cage? That is dangerous magic of the most sinister sort, Seth. If you want a word of advice, don't mention that to anyone,' she hissed. 'Not if your defence is the line that you know nothing about magic.' Angelique held the cane to his throat a few seconds longer, her eyes glinting dangerously, then dropped it back just enough to allow Seth to breathe.

'It's not a line,' muttered Seth, rubbing his neck. 'I know nothing about magic. What is one anyway?' He was guessing it had nothing to do with the beautiful lightning bugs that lived in the forest. She had looked truly terrified.

A shudder running through her, Angelique snapped the top of her cane shut. 'You really don't want to know. Sometimes magic can be . . .' she paused and looked as if she was having difficulty finding just the right word '. . . some magic can be horrible.'

Just for a moment, learning that magic was real had been a wondrous, fantastical discovery. Now Seth wasn't so sure.

'Won't look good for your defence if Kingfisher finds you wandering about,' said Angelique, pointing with her cane. 'You probably need some help getting back into the cupboard.'

'I can do it myself,' said Seth.

She followed him back downstairs anyway, this time the lobby was thankfully empty and he crawled into the darkness. Only hours ago, his life had seemed tough coping with Tiffany's vile scheming. Now he was accused, not just of murder, but of murdering the most important sorcerer in the land.

He would rather stay here and suffer at Tiffany's evil hands for ever rather than be taken away with everyone believing he'd murdered Dr Thallomius, who had only been kind to Seth.

But what was he going to do? He was way out of his depth here.

'By the way, which guest mentioned a firefly cage?' she asked before she shut him back into the darkness.

She'd made an attempt to sound casual, but Seth knew she was really interested in the answer.

'Sorry, I don't remember.'

'Well, Seth, I suggest you try just a bit harder to find some answers if you want to get yourself out of this mess. If you want my advice, find out how someone could have got into that locked dining room to poison the pudding. That's the key. That's how you save yourself.' He heard her sigh. 'But right now I have two problems.'

Seth felt like answering that he was facing a lot more than two problems. He didn't have a clue what she was up to, prodding into everything with that dangerous cane and making the walls rumble. He certainly didn't trust her at all.

'OK,' he said reluctantly. 'Anything I can help with?'

'Well, Seth – you've lived here all your life and that puts me in a really awkward position.'

'Sorry to hear it,' he muttered.

'Because it could well be that you are the only one who can possibly help me here. But I have to agree with Kingfisher – you, Seth, are definitely far and away the mostly likely person to have killed Dr Thallomius.' And with that, she slammed the cupboard door and Seth was alone once more.

## 16. HE WASN'T READY

It felt like only seconds later when there came the scrape of the key in the lock and Angelique peered into the darkness of the cupboard. 'I said I'd come and fetch you. Someone from MagiCon has arrived. Your interrogation is about to begin.'

'Already?' Seth gulped and could not stop his insides quivering like blancmange.

He followed, dragging his feet, trying to find a brave face, one that would conceal his terror. He really wasn't ready for this. He needed to find something, anything, to say when they accused him of murdering Dr Thallomius.

'Please,' he said in a small voice as they reached the door to the tiny writing room adjoining the dining room. 'Is there anyone you can think of who would want to kill Dr Thallomius?'

Angelique turned as she gripped the door handle, her dark eyes flashed. Her answer was totally unexpected. 'Well, lots of people, I suppose.'

'Lots of people?' echoed Seth. That lovely little old man who had reminded him of Father Christmas and had given him a gold coin? 'Really? Like who?'

'As head of the Elysee he was bringing radical reforms. It made him enemies.'

'Enemies?' Seth tried not to cling too tightly to this sliver of unexpected hope. 'Anyone in particular?' It was difficult to think of that short and kindly man as someone who had enemies. Could one of these enemies be here right now, inside the hotel?

'Red Valerian has been causing heaps of trouble lately. He's suspected of being behind the death of two sorcerers only last week. And his followers are growing. Just tell the truth, Seth. Sure you'll be fine.'

Angelique knocked on the door and opened it a crack to let those inside know Seth was waiting.

She left the door just ajar and hovered, which she must have done deliberately because she didn't even hide that she was putting her ear to the crack. Seth too, listened in. There were two voices.

'And as you are in charge of Security for Dr Thallomius's visit here,' Seth heard a voice say. 'You can help with something I'm most curious about. What on earth even brought him to this remote hotel?'

'Part of Dr Thallomius's recruitment drive to the Elysee,' explained the second voice, which Seth instantly recognized as Kingfisher's. 'It was a meeting for the Prospect, sir. All the latest hopefuls of officially joining the Elysee are here.'

Recruitment to the Elysee? Seth was slowly understanding. That list which had been in Dr Thallomius's room had referred to the Prospect. So this was what was behind the secretive feast and the strange procedures? This was what had brought all the strange guests here to the Last Chance Hotel?

They all wanted to be officially part of the magical world and they were going through some sort of application process?

'But it's murder, sir. Luckily we have a clear suspect. I wasn't in favour of you being bothered,' went on Kingfisher.

'I'm not bothered.'

'Poisoning by the kitchen boy. Could not be more straightforward.'

'Glad to hear it. When you called, I was in the middle of the deciding set of a tennis match with Andreas Phist. Sounds like I can get back to it. So, this kitchen boy slipped a fatal poison into the dessert of the head of the Elysee and we can all go home. Have I got it right?'

'Exactly. I have established the clear fact that he's the only person who had the opportunity to introduce the fatal poison into Dr Thallomius's food,' explained Kingfisher. 'So it simply must have been him. Let me arrest him now, you can get back to your tennis,' said Kingfisher smoothly. 'Although won't you have lost already?'

'Stranger things have happened. It was my serve as well. This is excellent work, Mr Fishfinger. I shall put that in my report. No one else could possibly have done it, eh? What a most intriguing case. I guess we should meet this kitchen boy should we? This killer kitchen boy. Right. I am ready to meet our master criminal.'

## 17. WE MAKE CRIMINALS DISAPPEAR

The door opened to the smallest room in the hotel. Kingfisher dragged Seth in and shoved him into one of four chairs gathered around a desk under the only lamp in the room, which cast a dim light.

Gregorian Kingfisher sat in the chair next to him. Seth darted a swift look at the person standing across the desk from them in the shadows, a man so tall he made the tiny writing room feel even smaller.

The person who was going to interrogate him.

Seth felt sweat trickle down the back of his neck.

In the gloom, it was impossible to make out much more than a very tall man with a head of silvery-grey hair and a long face. It was difficult to read his expression, as the weak light from the lamp reflected off of his little round glasses.

Seth gripped the arms of his chair as a long, uncomfortable silence developed. The tall man drummed his fingers on the desk.

After what seemed like minutes had ticked by, Seth began to fear no one was even going to bother asking him questions. Everyone just thought he was guilty. The man from MagiCon wasn't even going to give him a chance to explain.

Then the finger-drumming stopped.

'I'd like to hear more about this fascinatingly routine visit by Dr Thallomius,' he said, addressing Kingfisher. 'Routine. Ah yes, apart from the murder. Unless I've missed something, that doesn't usually happen at a Prospect. What does Security say about that – ah, that's you, isn't it, Mr Fishfinger.'

'My name is Kingfisher, sir, Gregorian Kingfisher.'

'Of course it is. So, the moment the dessert left the kitchen it was taken to the dining room?'

'It was. The five-minute warning was given once all the food was assembled for the Feast, following all the correct procedures. The door was locked.'

'And after five minutes, the door was opened again?' asked the tall man.

'During that five minutes no one could have got into the dining room,' insisted Kingfisher. 'When the door was unlocked everyone sat down to eat. Angelique Squerr was sitting next to that dessert right until the moment Dr Thallomius ate it. I questioned everyone. She is adamant no one could have touched it.'

'Well, well, I believe that gives us just two intriguing possibilities. Maybe three.' The man leant forward and completely unexpectedly shook Seth's hand.

'Inspector Pewter, MagiCon. For all your magical crime solving needs. You'll have heard of us, of course. I would like to say that most of the rumours really aren't true.'

'No, sir,' Seth managed to squeak, wiping his sweating hands on his trousers and fighting an urge to introduce himself to this magical inspector as the main suspect.

Kingfisher gave Seth a triumphant glance and Seth could feel his future slipping away. He braced himself finally for questions, the back of his neck prickling.

Pewter cleared his throat with a discreet cough

and Seth guessed this was it, the questions were coming.

'Do you play tennis?' Pewter asked.

Seth shook his head nervously, his voice seemed to have deserted him. He was focused on Pewter being part of the magical police and having all sorts of unusual and unpleasant methods for extracting the truth.

'Very wise,' nodded Pewter. 'Ridiculous game. But somewhat addictive.' He let out a deep sigh. 'You think you're getting better, but—'

'The poison wasn't in it when it went into the dining room,' said Seth, speaking quickly, but the words coming out as a whisper. 'I had no reason to kill him. He was kind to me.'

'Was he indeed?' Pewter inched the top half of his body across the desk so his head was level with Seth's. 'Quiet for one who's causing all the trouble. When you said "No, sir" a moment ago, did you mean you had never heard of MagiCon, or just had never heard the rumours?'

'Err, both, sir.'

'Well, well. Now that leads me on to a most important question.' He looked about him, his head almost scraping the ceiling. 'Do you think there's any chance of a cup of tea?' He looked at Kingfisher.

'And have you offered one to your master criminal?'

'Erm . . .' faltered Kingfisher.

Pewter rummaged in an inside pocket and Seth took the small, plain white card he slid across the desk. He read the words, which were arranged in a circle: *MagiCon – all your magical crimes SOLVED*.

Alongside the words was a picture of Pewter looking like a headmaster about to dish out an awful punishment.

'We used to have this slogan *we make crime disappear* – you've heard of that? It was quite famous at one time.'

'I – I don't think so, sir.'

'It was a rubbish slogan anyway, I mean, no one can make crime disappear. We make criminals disappear, occasionally.' His face broke into a smile. 'But we do bring them back again – well,' the smile fell again, 'most of them.'

Seth noticed that after the word SOLVED was a small asterisk and at the bottom of the card in tiny letters was the word *usually*.

'What does this mean – usually?' asked Seth, frowning at the card. 'Solved – usually?'

'Oh, don't worry about that,' said Pewter, taking the card back and tucking it in an inside jacket pocket and revealing a range of miniature bottles and jars along the lining as he did so. 'That's just something overcautious legal folk advised to put in after the incident with the werewolf and the piano player. If you ask me, things didn't end as badly for that werewolf as people say.'

There was a soft tap at the door and Angelique slipped in without waiting to be asked. 'Angelique Squerr,' she announced. 'I was Dr Thallomius's personal assistant. I took notes at the Prospect. I thought there might be something I could help with?' She took a seat at the desk.

'Perfect timing, Miss Squerr. We were discussing what exactly brought the Sorcerer General himself to the Last Chance Hotel. I am sure you are going to tell us that Thallomius himself came all the way out here to meet exceptional candidates. Ones he was keen to invite into the magical community? Strong signs of magic?'

Angelique twirled the long strand of red in her hair around and around her fingers. 'Not particularly.'

'Not particularly. I see.'

Seth kept his fingers clenched on the arms of the chair, trying not to panic as he waited for someone to tell him whether he was under arrest or not. Four people in the minuscule room meant all of them were practically touching noses and the heat was soaring now. If he didn't get out of here soon, he felt he was going to faint or start to blurt out the wrong things.

He looked up as a gust of fresh air breathed into the room, carrying with it an aroma of the hotel's signature fish-head soup. Pewter had opened the door and now he lifted his nose and sniffed. 'What is that delicious smell?'

'That's soup, sir,' replied Seth, always more confident talking about anything to do with cooking.

'Soup? Well, I have just been playing the most intense tennis of my life. I don't know about everyone else, but might I suggest we move somewhere a little more roomy? And if possible, our chief murder suspect could make himself useful and lead us to this soup.'

Seth went to rise and gratefully abandon the stifling room when he felt a hand on his shoulder. He looked up into Pewter's serious face towering above him.

'Unless you have got something you want to tell me, young Seth?'

Seth caught a whiff of clean mintiness as Pewter put his face even closer.

'You're not going to warn me not to eat that soup, are you?' Pewter said in a low voice.

'N-no, sir. Not at all, sir. The soup is very good, sir. My father's recipe.'

'And you are completely sure you didn't poison the soup as well as that apricot dessert?'

Seth swallowed, then shook his head firmly. 'Sir, I didn't poison anything.'

As he looked fearfully into the inspector's face, Seth thought he saw wrinkles appearing in the corners of Pewter's eyes, as though his face might be crinkling into the ghost of a mischievous smile.

But Seth thought he may have simply imagined it as he scrambled gratefully out of his seat, relieved to lead the way to the kitchen in search of soup.

## 18. UP TO HIS ELBOWS IN TROUBLE

In the kitchen, a few moments later, Seth was sliding a bowl in front of Inspector Pewter and stuttering reassuring words about the safety of the soup. He was telling him that the soup had been eaten by many of the guests that evening with no ill effects, when Dunster-Dunstable bustled in. He looked directly at Seth with blatant curiosity, and then scuttled over to Angelique and Kingfisher.

'So, what happens now?' Dunster-Dunstable muttered, as he took a pack of cards out of his pocket and started shuffling them. 'I mean, it's a tricky one isn't it? Dr Thallomius won't be able to tell us – did we all pass – are we in the Elysee? What's going to happen to us?'

He kept sliding glances towards Seth, who was so used to being either ignored or bossed around, it felt weird to be the centre of attention. He took a seat in the darkest and farthest corner.

Angelique rose and looked down her long nose. 'Dr Thallomius is dead. Murdered. That is surely all anyone is thinking of right now.'

Inspector Pewter went over and gripped Dunster-Dunstable's hand warmly. 'The Great Gandolfini. Amazing stage illusions. You've been performing since you were eight, I believe? Inspector Pewter, MagiCon – you've heard of us of course. Now, we have here a devilishly clever crime, no one can see how it was done, so blame has fallen on this roguish kitchen boy. Impossible crime, utterly fascinating locked-room mystery. Seems right up your street. Bet you have ideas?' Pewter raised one of his silvery eyebrows.

Dunster-Dunstable looked flattered, then his expression changed. He placed both his hands on his chest and looked wounded. 'You can't think I had anything to do with it? What reason would I have to kill him? He was just about to finally award me my rightful place in the Elysee.'

Angelique's calm voice carried from the back of the kitchen, 'Or maybe not. Maybe you weren't happy that this is the third time you've auditioned for the Prospect. Maybe you thought he'd reject you again.'

'Worried Dr Thallomius would see straight through your cheap tricks? Going by the ludicrous name of the Great Gandolfini,' scoffed Kingfisher. 'Nothing but smoke and mirrors. Did you fail again to do any genuine magic?'

'So this is what happens now is it? We all sit around and accuse each other?' Dunster-Dunstable moved towards Kingfisher, his face dropping its grin, but only for a second, then his mischievous smile was back in its proper place. 'Well, this time my magic was awesome. This time I am bound to be in.' He put his head on one side. 'But, perhaps I should just say, do you know what a proper old state Papperspook got into when she found out Dr Thallomius himself was taking the Prospect? Of course, Gloria's grandfather – Wintergreen Troutbean – and Dr Thallomius fell out big time. Bad blood with Thallomius goes back years. And why don't you ask the professor what she thinks of the Prospect?'

Kingfisher leapt in. 'Bad blood?'

Seth was listening to everything, but all he could think, with a sinking feeling, was that this was going to keep happening. People were going to talk about things that were way beyond him. Things that made no sense about a world of which he knew nothing.

'Didn't you know that the last anyone heard of Wintergreen was that he was one of the Missing Feared Exploded as a result of the Unpleasant?' went on Darinder, as he spun out of the room with a mischievous grin on his face and left Seth puzzling further.

Seth sat in his quiet corner realizing that he had a desperate need to find out more. Pewter and Kingfisher were talking in low voices, exchanging notes, and Angelique was staring into the far distance, letting her tea go cold.

He needed to find out everything he could about the magical world, because his only chance of proving that he was innocent was to find out who had really done it. And to do that he needed to understand. The only hope he had was to remain as quiet as possible, to keep listening and maybe just see if Angelique would tell him just a little bit more.

There was a noise from just outside the room. A laugh that sounded exactly like the bark of a dog.

Seth tensed at the sound, which probably meant Tiffany had been delighting in listening to someone else tormenting Seth for a change and now she was here to stir things up.

Seth heard the dread sound of her tiny footsteps as she made her entrance into the kitchen, bestowing one of her dazzling smiles on everyone in turn.

'This tragedy is so shocking,' she began in a low, breathy voice. 'I just wanted you all to know that I would be more than delighted to do whatever I can to help.'

Tiffany's white face loomed behind Seth as she inched closer to where he was sitting in his chair. How long had she been lurking? Long enough to have found out that their murdered VIP guest was the most important sorcerer in the land?

He couldn't even begin to imagine how Tiffany would react to that news or what she might do if she found out that all the people staying at the hotel were here to apply to join the magical community.

He fervently hoped she was still in the dark about it all, because Tiffany having the power of magic was one of the worst things he could possibly imagine. Something so terrifying, worse, even, than being led away from here in handcuffs.

She blinked her blue eyes and went and stood

right behind Seth's chair. 'I want to help to clear up this terrible crime.'

'How kind of you to offer,' declared Pewter. 'Delightful! Perfect timing to be of help. You are just the person we need to help us clear up a confusion. I am intrigued by this famous dessert that was clearly marked as intended only for Dr Thallomius?'

'I was asked to do something special just for him,' said Seth nervously, but glad of a chance to explain. 'There was something in the other dessert he was allergic to.'

'See, he even researched his victim!' snapped Kingfisher.

'Err, well, it's important to know things about the guests,' stammered Seth.

'And the second Dr Thallomius ate this dessert, he dropped down, quite dead?' went on Pewter.

Seth nodded.

'Are you going to arrest my little saucepan scrubber?' Tiffany's beautiful face adopted a mask of concern, but Seth could tell she was gleeful. 'You're really going to take him away? I can't imagine Seth doing anything quite so daring, I mean, so disturbing, as murdering someone. Surely he is going back to his bins and his washing up?'

Tiffany had moved even closer to Seth's chair

now, so that he could almost smell her delight as she leant forward, her breath tickling as she spoke right in his ear.

She turned to Pewter and said sweetly. 'So what can I do? There must be something.'

'Well yes. I am sure it must have been you who created this stunning pavlova I've been hearing about? And the apricot dessert, your work I am sure? Not the work of your little saucepan scrubber here?'

Tiffany turned around slowly, giving Pewter the full benefit of her hypnotic eyes. 'Oh, I'm afraid all of that was Seth. He is a very slow learner and more than a little useless, but I have done my best to teach him a thing or two when I can spare the time. And I have had a little success. You may need to press him a little to confess. I am sure I could help with that too. In fact, I'd be delighted.'

The familiar terrifying smell of stale rum announced the arrival of Norrie Bunn. Was she here to torment him like her daughter? Was no one going to stand up for Seth and point out he had no reason to kill Dr Thallomius?

'I think you have questioned Seth long enough,' said Norrie, and just for a moment Seth thought he saw a glimmer of salvation. 'He has duties that he is very behind with. Unless you are arresting him and taking him away tonight, I suggest he goes and tidies up the hotel lounge and makes it fit for guests. And stoke up the fire while you are about it, Seth.'

# 19. A Genius Inventor

In the lounge, sitting quite alone, huddled in the chair nearest to the fireplace, with only the last red flickering of the dwindling fire for company, sat Count Marred.

He looked the picture of misery as Seth slipped in and gathered together the glasses and wiped the low table by the squashy chairs. Count Boldo Marred barely looked up to register his presence as Seth silently cleared the cocktail bar from when everyone had been in here only a few hours ago, sharing drinks and nervous jokes and playing a jolly game of cards.

The Count was still lost in a world of his own as others joined him in the comfortable chairs and Norrie began to offer drinks from the bar.

But when Seth went to stoke the fire, he felt Count Marred's intense scrutiny and was glad when Kingfisher broke the silence that had developed, even though what he said only reminded Seth of the fact that he had a head swimming with questions.

'My background checks mean I can confirm it is true,' Kingfisher announced officiously. 'Wintergreen Troutbean, Gloria Troutbean's grandfather, is indeed one of the sorcerers officially declared Missing Feared Exploded following that terrible day that everyone fears even to talk about.'

'Ah yes, Wintergreen was indeed one of the lost of the Unpleasant.' It was Count Marred who spoke, growling low in his gravelly voice. 'That day brought such appalling loss of life among members of our community. A tragedy.'

Kingfisher carried on reading his notes. 'And Wintergreen was once a close friend of Dr Thallomius. They were famous for their magical inventions.'

'Such a genius inventor in his younger days – people have forgotten,' sighed Count Marred. 'But I never heard Torpor speak a bad word against Wintergreen Troutbean. It is true that they fell out. But that was donkey's years ago.'

'Ah well, Dr Thallomius probably knew better than anyone how nothing annoys one's enemies quite so much as forgiving them,' said Pewter, sinking into a seat alongside him. 'Boldo, you were great friends with Dr Thallomius. I am extremely sorry for your loss. You spent the afternoon with him. Did he say anything to you that might help us?'

Boldo shook his head slowly. 'Torpor was right as rain all afternoon. We had tea and then played a jolly game of four-handed brag. Torpor was beating us all, although that was Dunster-Dunstable up to his old tricks. Devil with a pack of cards that boy.'

'But Dr Thallomius was winning all the money,' Kingfisher frowned.

Marred spread his hands. 'Of course. That lad was making sure Dr Thallomius won – because it was a clumsy attempt at a bribe! Not that it would have made the slightest bit of difference. Torpor took his duties too seriously. Saving the magical world from dwindling and dying out, that was Torpor. A life spent fighting for magic to be a force for good.'

Marred's scarred face crumpled into a picture of

misery. 'Can you credit it, Pewter, that our world has grown so fragile that there are actually people out there who do not believe magical people exist? My good friend Thallomius was determined to change that. There have been some dark times.' Count Marred burst into tears, but carried on bravely. 'But this idea of seeking out those with true magic and inviting them to become apprentices. Genius. And essential to the future health of the world of sorcerers, wasn't it, Pewter?'

'Brave policies,' said Pewter.

Marred took the large tartan handkerchief Pewter offered him and wiped a big tear from the corner of his eye. 'Torpor was not afraid to take them on. Sorcerers were coming around to recognize that his was the way forward.'

'Although,' interrupted Gregorian Kingfisher smoothly, 'people do have a habit of blaming his policies for the uprising that resulted in the Unpleasant and the unfortunate ends of those forty-two sorcerers now Missing Feared Exploded.'

Boldo looked aghast for a moment, then his face became thoughtful. 'You believe the sinister hand of Red Valerian must somehow have reached even into this isolated wood? His forces are growing, I know. How do we catch that villain?'

Kingfisher shook his head. 'The killer is among us.' He looked pointedly at Seth.

As Seth crouched to put on another log, the flames leapt up and the dark dome of Count Marred's bald head reflected the glow of the firelight as he wiped away another tear. And a small treacherous voice whispered what great cover it would be if he had murdered Thallomius himself.

Seth hated himself for even thinking it.

Marred was genuinely upset. And what reason would he have? It sounded like Dr Thallomius was a wonderful person. Opening up the magical world for apprentices? That sounded beyond wonderful.

'Inspector Pewter, the hotel could be full of people who had very good reasons to kill Dr Thallomius,' snapped Kingfisher, darting another threatening look at Seth. 'But let's not lose sight of the fact that only one could have slipped him the poison. Sir.'

'I guess it just goes to show that at an early stage of the investigation it's often difficult to know what the right clues are likely to be,' replied Pewter thoughtfully.

Seth felt a warm hand on his shoulder. He stared up at Pewter, shrinking at the thought that he was about to be led off to spend an uncomfortable night locked in that broom cupboard.

'Noticed you didn't serve up yourself any soup, Seth. Not hungry?'

Seth heard his stomach grumble.

'I always find I get the best cooperation from employers with tricky deaths on their premises. Otherwise cases can drag on for weeks and be investigated very shoddily. I feel sure Mr Bunn can spare you a bowl of soup.'

Pewter led him back to the silent kitchen and Seth was shocked afresh to see the state of devastation and wearily started to tackle a puddle of spilt sauce on the floor and the overflowing bins. Crusted pans were piled high next to the sink and it was difficult to know even where to start when he found himself being steered to a chair and a bowl put in front of him.

Seth took up a spoon and began to eat, uncomfortable under Pewter's intense gaze.

Pewter helped himself to more soup and joined Seth at the table. 'You were right about this soup. Now, are you going to make a dash through this forest in the middle of the night?'

Seth shook his head. 'I'm not going anywhere. Except maybe to jail, if Mr Kingfisher has his way.'

'Leaving Mr Kingfisher's wishes aside for the

moment, I'm sure you have thoughts about this murder?'

Seth swallowed another mouthful of soup.

It seemed there was hope that there might be people who had reasons for wanting Dr Thallomius dead – and some of them right here in the hotel. Yet it all came back to the fact that no one had a chance to poison the dessert. Seth simply could not puzzle that out.

He looked at Pewter and wished he knew what he was thinking. All he could hope was that there was room for doubt that a boy who knew nothing about the magical world was really the most likely suspect for murdering Dr Thallomius.

'I do have a few questions.'

'Hit me with one.'

'There is one odd thing I have been wondering about. I was told to lay a table for eight, yet there were only seven guests.'

Pewter looked at him for so long Seth thought he'd gone into a trance. Had he said the wrong thing?

Eventually Pewter said, 'Another guest expected for the Prospect? One we don't yet know about? I have to say, I find this case gets more and more intriguing. Now, I have a question for you.'

Seth heard himself sigh. He'd known there would

be questions. Had Pewter deliberately waited until he was so tired he felt he was bound to easily wrong-foot him?

'Would you ever leave?'

'Leave?' said Seth, startled by another unexpected turn in the questions. He tried to imagine being anywhere else but here – and failed. Part of him longed to see the world beyond the Last Hope Forest – at least he thought he did. But it was a vast, unknown place. His insides curled like paper in flame at the thought. 'I've no friends, no relations, no money.'

'Then that would take a certain kind of bravery. Would be a whole lot riskier than staying. So . . . any final thoughts that might shed some light on this tragedy?' said Pewter.

Seth wished he could come up with something, anything, that might explain what had happened and didn't point directly to him.

'I know it looks like an impossible crime, sir,' he said falteringly. 'No one can explain how the poison got into that dessert. I am totally at a loss to understand how it happened. It wasn't me. My only thought is that . . . could the murderer— I mean, could someone have used magic somehow to kill Dr Thallomius? Otherwise it really does seem impossible. But it happened.'

Pewter looked at him so long and so steadily Seth thought he'd gone into a trance again. Seth had the feeling he'd asked a very stupid question.

'*When you have eliminated the impossible, whatever remains, however improbable, must be the truth.*' said Pewter. 'Heard that before? Was said by a detective quite possibly even more famous than me.'

'That was said by Sherlock Holmes, sir,' said Seth. 'But I've never understood – what does it mean exactly?'

'I think it means that your father must have had a good nose and that he passed it on to you. I mean – I like to think I have a good nose myself, although not for knowing when a recipe is just right. They say I have a nose for trouble. And for lies and evasions.'

'That's three things,' said Seth.

'Ah yes. But my nose is most famous for being able to detect one important thing – magic. And if there is one thing my nose is telling me, Seth, it is that you are right. There is magic, right here in the very heart of this seemingly impossible crime.'

## 20. A Search by Torchlight

He was so tired his bones ached, but Seth could only toss and turn in his narrow bed, unable to sleep.

With everything else that had happened, the one thought that kept him awake most of all was not the one he thought he would find himself thinking about.

Magic was real.

Yet it was a bit like stepping through a door and arriving in an unexpected yet beautiful place, only to be instantly told that here lurked something dark, dangerous and unknowable. Angelique had scared him with how she'd reacted when he'd mentioned the dark magic of the firefly cage.

He fidgeted and earned himself a sharp claw from Nightshade, who was curled, as usual, at the end of his bed. He tried to lie still.

Seth wanted to stroke her soft fur, but he didn't want to wake her. He simply loved the fact that she had decided to reveal to him that she could talk. How lucky was he to have a cat that could talk? OK, it would have been lovely to have had her to talk things over with during the last couple of years, which had been lonely. But she had always been there for him. And he feared if he asked her why she'd kept it a secret, she might simply go back to being silent again. She was pretty grumpy. He'd never expected just how grumpy.

He should focus on making sense of conversations roaming his head, to try to piece together what possibly could have happened.

How had the poison got into that dessert? Pewter was right that it seemed the most impossible, unanswerable question. But it had happened. He had to work it out. How else was he going to clear his name?

Who had killed Dr Thallomius? Was he anywhere near knowing?

That name – Red Valerian – had come quickly to Angelique when he had asked who might want Dr Thallomius dead. But it had to be someone inside the hotel. Seth's mind refused to stop racing over everything that had happened and his desperate need to work out the truth kept him tossing and turning.

Darinder Dunster-Dunstable floated into view as effortlessly as a balloon, reaching behind Seth's ear and triumphantly waving aloft the beautiful stemmed dessert bowl.

Angelique loomed towards him, the deadly end of her cane pointing directly at this throat. *It's an impossible crime, Seth, and you are the prime suspect.*

Pewter was towering over Seth, more treelike than ever – he even had branches sprouting out of his head, like antlers.

And then Seth was peering between bars, trapped in a dark place, imprisoned in a tiny cage, despairing. He felt he had been here his whole life with no hope of rescue and as he shook the bars of his prison something was stabbing his leg and tugging painfully at his hair.

Seth blinked open his eyes.

'You were screaming,' said Nightshade.

'I was? Sorry. Didn't even realize I'd fallen asleep.'

Nightshade gave a full stretch and clawed at the scratchy blanket. 'Come on, which of them did it?'

'I don't know. How can I work it out?'

'Come on Seth, concentrate. What about that one going around the hotel with the dangerous cane? Don't trust her an inch. Or that small tricksy kid with the pointy ears. He's good at making things appear from nowhere. Or that friend with the scar. I watched him for ages in the lounge. Trying to look upset.'

'I think he was upset,' said Seth. 'Count Marred wasn't faking, I'm sure.'

But was he really sure?

Someone here was lying.

Seth chewed everything over. 'They all seem up to no good. Dunster-Dunstable was trying to bribe Dr Thallomius. Gloria's grandfather is someone who is apparently Missing Feared Exploded after this terrible event that they call the Unpleasant. Apparently Wintergreen Troutbean and Dr Thallomius were once inventor friends back in the time when Dr Thallomius created magical science devices, but they fell out. And I could tell instantly Professor Papperspook hated Dr Thallomius.'

'Have you worked out why?'

'I think it's because there are troubles in the magical world,' said Seth thoughtfully. 'Angelique mentioned something about reforms. Dr Thallomius was opening up the magical world, giving new recruits a chance to join.'

'Well that sounds great.'

'Yes, that's what I thought. But not everyone is in favour and it sounds like it led to this great battle, the Unpleasant, where a lot of sorcerers died. No one is even sure who actually did die in it. Angelique said Dr Thallomius had enemies.'

'Sounds grim.'

'He brought in these brave policies because there are now so few magical people about that the magical world is in danger of dying out,' said Seth, lost in his own thoughts for a moment. 'I didn't even know about the magical world a few hours ago. Now it seems terrible to think magical people might become extinct.'

'Seth, you're getting distracted again. OK. What else have you learnt?'

'Basically, that's what everyone is here for – the honour of being officially invited into the Elysee. You can become an apprentice if you can prove you have some spark of magic and that's not always found in people from magical families. But I think proving it is difficult.' Seth tickled her under the chin.

'But how was he poisoned, Seth?'

'That is a big question. Angelique says I have answers, but she's wrong.' Seth tugged at his hair.

'But you must have some idea, Seth,' Nightshade snuggled further into Seth's lap. 'My money is on that Gloria with the sour face. A long-standing grudge between her family and Thallomius sounds a good enough reason to top him.' Nightshade gave a long, slow stretch. 'So which of 'em was it? Tell me, then I can go back to sleep.'

He tipped her to the floor. 'Trouble is, I just don't know. Perhaps the answer is staring at us.'

'Great to hear it! I tried to get under every table to listen and I've absolutely no idea! Is it that sour-faced girl? She looks the sort who could ruin a perfectly good pudding just by looking at it. And what about that eighth seat at the table?'

Her gaze followed Seth as he grabbed his torch and jacket. 'Oh no, don't tell me it involves heading outside. It's perishing out there. You know what the frost does to my fur. Can't it wait until the sun's up?'

'No. This really can't wait. There really is only one

person who could have killed Dr Thallomius.'

'Let's get 'em. Who is it?'

'Trouble is, Nightshade – what if it actually was me?'

## 21. The Smell of Almonds

'Whiskers and white mice,' growled Nightshade. 'Of course it wasn't you. You're off out to find evidence against yourself? What a brilliant idea. Mind if I don't come?'

But she didn't leap back on to her warm patch on the bed, just slunk alongside him as they both made their way down the rickety stairs, pausing on the second-floor landing to listen to Norrie Bunn safely snoring. Nightshade sped ahead, the darkness swallowing her up and not bothering her in the slightest.

Seth made sure he avoided treading on the creaky third step from the top and safely reached the ground floor.

The hotel was in silence, apart from the ticking of the grandfather clock in the hall which showed it was already nearly morning.

'The door from the lounge into the garden opens the quietest,' suggested Nightshade. 'Everyone's asleep, but I can double check the coast is clear.' She shot through Seth's legs. Two seconds later she was back. 'Guess what – door's already open – and old Bunn is such a stickler for locking everything up at night. We'd best go careful. There's a murderer on the loose.'

'Thanks Nightshade.'

Seth lifted his nose to see if he could detect any clues in the air about who else might be prowling in the night ahead of them. Nightshade plunged on like liquid darkness and when Seth stepped outside, the light from his torch barely penetrated the inky black.

They moved swiftly under the canopy of trees, which blotted out any helpful twinkling of starlight and even the hopeless slip of moon. With just the torchlight, Seth picked his way as they headed in the direction of the glow-worm glade. Beyond that was a fierce loop of river that enclosed the grounds of the hotel, guarded by a waterfall, which cut off travel to the north.

'I did everything exactly as Kingfisher said,' he whispered. 'I made that dessert, no one else touched it and then it was whisked into the dining room, which was locked. No one could have poisoned it.'

'So someone used magic to get into the dining room.'

Seth strode on. 'I was tired and in a hurry,' he said grimly. 'I made that dessert. What if I picked something by accident, something like belladonna, and it got mixed up with the other ingredients, Nightshade? It *is* possible.'

'Possible, but unlikely. Did the poison smell like belladonna?'

Seth thought back to the dining room. 'It smelt more like almonds.'

'Well then, that's a big clue. No one knows more than you about ingredients. Now, I bet that smell wasn't in the dessert when you took it into the dining room.'

'But I have to be sure,' said Seth stubbornly.

'Stop blaming yourself, Seth. It wasn't you.'

Guests muttered about the spookiness of the wet, windy woods that grew almost to the door of the hotel. It was easy to imagine faces in the trunks of the trees. You often came across a pair of unseeing eyes or a gaping mouth and realized it was an old statue, overgrown with ivy and spotted with yellow lichen.

Seth remembered exactly the steps he'd traced on his quest for apricots. He hadn't known where they grew, yet he'd known for sure they'd be there. It was strange, but the garden was like that. Whatever the season, if you needed a recipe, even one that involved both peaches and pumpkins, you headed into the garden and you would eventually find what you needed. Sometimes, when he was younger, Seth had convinced himself that the garden was magic.

Resentment laced every delicate step Nightshade took across the frosty ground, moving so it looked as if her paws hardly made contact with the earth. They passed what had once been a great greenhouse, now scarred with jagged windows. Inside grew a giant tree whose branches looked like the clawing fingers of a desperate prisoner reaching through the broken glass to freedom.

'Doing this in the dark wasn't such a bright idea,' muttered Nightshade.

'Great. Everyone's a critic,' said Seth. 'You didn't have to come.'

She muttered something under her breath.

There was only the sound of Seth's feet crunching noisily on the twigs and leaves, the scent of moist earth and the fresh sharp tang of early icy air filling his nostrils.

He stumbled over a tree root, twisting his ankle. He hobbled onwards.

'Come on. Nearly there.' Nightshade brushed past his legs and leapt forwards into the darkness.

Seth took a deep breath, stumbling forwards and at last, even in the dark, they were at the place, exactly as he remembered. There were the apricots.

Nightshade lifted her nose in the night air. 'Get on with it, Seth, we'll get frostbite out here.'

'If I made a terrible mistake, I shall own up.' Seth gripped the torch firmly.

Nightshade looked up at him, her big eyes reflecting the thin moonlight. 'Then I guess we're all doomed.'

'Thanks Nightshade.' Seth wondered if he would ever get used to her talking. 'You are such a comfort.'

As he pushed aside the foliage, his heart was hammering as he expected to catch sight of something deadly curling around the fruit, or a lethal dark berry in just the wrong place waiting to drop him into trouble.

The first ghostly light of dawn breaking helped his search, warming to a cheerful flush of pink on the horizon.

'There's nothing, Nightshade,' Seth breathed. 'Just the apricots.'

Seth felt his heart lift.

'OK, sound detective work,' said Nightshade, 'but I knew from the start that dessert simply could not have been poisoned when it left the kitchen.'

The relief was so great it made his steps light as they turned back to the hotel.

'Thanks, Nightshade. You were absolutely right. I know now for sure.'

'You should listen to me. Seth, don't you remember? You missed the biggest clue. Like every good chef – you tasted that dessert yourself before it went into the dining room.'

Seth stopped. 'Oh, so I did.'

'If it was poisoned, Seth, you'd be dead. That proof enough for you? You're still walking about. Gotta get better with your detective work. You can't miss big clues like that,' she grouched.

'Well why didn't you say something before?' said Seth snappily.

'You were so keen to have a downer on yourself, thought you needed to get over beating yourself up.

Anyway, you done? Now p'raps we can focus on getting on the trail of whoever actually did it. We need to find out who's been using magic. Let's go! Let's find out who got into that dining room.'

## 22. Hunting for Birdsong

Nightshade switched the conversation to breakfast. And not just her own breakfast. She was really keen that Seth didn't get into big trouble with the Bunns for neglecting his duties. She reminded him that once they cleared his name, Seth was still going to have to keep on the Bunns' good side – if they had one.

They bickered cheerfully as they walked back, Nightshade resisting scampering after every low rustle in the leaves that potentially alerted her to a tasty breakfast. They were almost back at the hotel when she lifted her nose and paused.

Seth peered cautiously around and saw what Nightshade had seen – a figure in among the bushes. Someone else was up early. Someone who was doing something very strange indeed.

Seth risked stealing closer and was rewarded by a small chink of clear brightness in the slate-grey clouds gathered moodily on the horizon, revealing Professor Papperspook in all her gaudy glory. She was ambling through the rose garden, moving slowly and silently, but with a determined look on her face as if stalking something, her giant complicated bird's nest of hair gently bobbing. She was gripping a colossal net on a hoop.

'You think she's doing magic?' Seth whispered.

Nightshade muttered something about being less interested in magic than breakfast and scampered off in pursuit of some small, unsuspecting woodland creature.

An alarmed bird call sounded shrill on the sharp morning air and Professor Papperspook lifted her pointed nose and moved swiftly and surely towards the sound. She swiped her net then opened one of the crystal bottles Seth recognized from the case in her room. She stuffed something inside.

As another bird started its song her head lifted again, the net moved through the air as she pursued it with a determined look on her beaky features.

Seth, in spite of wanting to get back into the hotel and nervous of speaking to anyone, decided he'd try and find out what she was doing.

'Good morning, Professor Papperspook.'

She swung around, almost decapitating Seth with her net. But when she saw who it was she smiled.

'Wonderful woodland. Nothing but trees for absolutely miles.' She breathed the fresh air deeply through her nostrils.

'Most people complain about that actually.'

'Remarkable.' As the pink glow began to lift on the horizon, so the low chatter of birdsong started to grow. 'Would you like to help me to catch some birdsong? If I'm lucky I'll get a whole dawn chorus. Marvellous.'

'Me?' asked Seth, astonished. 'I . . . I'd love to. If you think I could.'

'Just step up quickly, grip right here, listen and swoop. Swoop!' The net was amazingly light, despite its size.

A startled blackbird yelled at him.

'No, not like you're catching tiddlers, like you're after a massive pike for your supper. Right! There you go! That's it!'

Seth did his best. The birds around him seemed to all be shouting at once. It was impossible to tell the cries apart. It was as if someone was conducting an orchestra and Professor Papperspook encouraged him to take swoop after swoop. She seized the net from him and pushed her large nose into it. 'I believe you got one.'

Seth watched as she poked the end of the net into a bottle.

'Did I really get something?'

'Yes, you got it, Seth.'

'Wow,' he said, remembering how he'd lifted that stopper in her room and that bird cry had flooded out. Just from a tiny bottle. Had he really just captured a sound like that? 'Magic is – well, it's awesome.'

'I do know my magic is very limited and of a very rare and particular kind,' the professor shrugged modestly. 'But sadly some people are quick to dismiss my life's work.'

'I think it's brilliant. Is it difficult to know if something is truly magic?' Kingfisher had sneered at Dunster-Dunstable's illusions as not being true magic. And everyone was here going through some sort of test to see if they could prove their magic.

She chuckled, making her second chin wobble. 'Well I can't walk into a room and create a fireball with my bare hands. Not like some people can. I can't even walk into a room and change a chair into a toadstool.'

'Can some people really do that?' asked Seth, wide-eyed.

'Magic tends to come to people differently.'

'It sounds brilliant for someone like Miss Trout-bean to be able to become an apprentice.'

Professor Papperspook's face lost its smile. 'It's a terrible insult.'

'B-but . . . it *is*? Scouring the country, trying to recruit people with a spark of magic? I . . . I thought Dr Thallomius's ideas sounded heroic.'

'Heroic?' Professor Papperspook's friendly manner completely disappeared. Even the birdsong net drooped. 'Opening the doors to fraudsters and chancers. Where will it end? And the worst of it is, that's not all he was doing.'

'Count Marred said he was trying to save the magical world,' floundered Seth.

Professor Papperspook took a step nearer, making her tower of colourful hair nod. 'Count Marred was duped.' She was distracted by taking a big swipe as the drumming of a woodpecker resounded, looked in frustration at her net, then poked her beaky nose closer to Seth's face. 'He was a terrible man.'

'What do you mean?'

She carried on, swishing her net more in anger than an attempt to catch something. 'Fair, he called it. Insulting, I call it. To put my best friend's lovely girl through that. Questioning Gloria's magical ability. Getting her to prove her rightful place in the Elysee. It's beyond offensive. I have a certain reputation in the magical world and I aim to do everything I can to make sure Gloria gets her rightful place.'

Seth began feeling he might have more than a glimmer of understanding. He was thinking he might be beginning to see many reasons why sorcerers might not have taken so kindly to Dr Thallomius's reforms. 'Both you and Count Marred are here to take part in the Prospect because you need to prove you are magic too?'

'My magic is subtle. It is difficult for even sorcerers to properly understand. To have to stand up and prove our magic!'

Then she let out a curse and examined the net closely. She bent low to some woody shrubs where the spiders' webs grew in huge numbers, large, dewy and sticky. She carefully removed one of the webs and attached it to her net, which Seth could now see was made entirely from spiders' webs.

Then she dived off to stalk in the direction of a spreading oak tree that was beginning to shed its leaves, muttering, 'I am not going to let anyone, least of all that terrible man, interfere with my chance with this dawn chorus. There was a pesky wood-pecker got away from me a moment ago. And if only nuthatches could be persuaded to be more talkative.'

Then she turned, saw Seth was still following, fascinated, and put something in his hand. 'Think you might want to find a better place for this.'

She closed his fingers over something bumpy and rough. He had hopes it might be a gift of a small capsule of birdsong. He would love that, but as she moved off with her net held high, he scrutinized the object and could see it was an unusual piece of wood. Actually, when he looked at it closely, it wasn't simply a piece of wood, but a large and very intri-guing nut, all knobbly, with an interesting grain.

You never knew what might be growing out here, but Seth had seen nothing like that before. Where had it come from?

He plunged on after her.

'It fell on me as I walked outside the lounge doors,' she said over her shoulder. 'Took me a moment to realize what it actually was. I guess someone,' she turned to wink at him, 'was trying to dispose of it, but it must have got lodged in the shrubbery.'

Seth looked back at the hotel, where a gnarled wisteria clung to the outside. But how had a large nut been in the shrubbery? It hadn't been growing there, surely? Could it have been dropped from one of the windows above?

Mr and Mrs Bunn and Henri were on the second floor directly above the lounge. Angelique Squerr and Kingfisher were in rooms below them. Next to those were two empty rooms. He looked again at the nut.

'Don't know how you did it, but well done. Trust me.' She winked once more. 'I won't say a word.' She tapped the side of her nose, still chuckling as she moved off to where the birdsong was loudest.

Why had the professor given it to him?

He wished he understood that wink.

## 23. A Glorious Shade of Forget-me-nots

Seth looked up and knew it was about to be that perfect moment when the rose-tinted light of the early dawn broke over the trees. Soon the whole sky would momentarily come alive like it was aflame, touched with the most beautiful shade of cerise, like strawberries changing to oranges.

Seth loved this time of day in the autumn when you could breathe the scent of fruit ripening in the air. Just for a few fleeting minutes, if you were lucky enough to catch it, the forest would wake under a

cloud of sleepy fog that would gradually lift, expos-
ing millions of leaves in a costume so different from
their summer green, it felt like a totally new place.
But that was the beauty of the forest. Every single
day he would see something fresh, it would change
hour by hour. Yet still somehow remain the same.

These days the hotel had become so quiet. The
only folk who strayed here were so utterly lost in the
Last Hope Forest they couldn't believe their luck to
stumble upon somewhere they'd get a welcome bed
and a late-night cup of cocoa.

But Seth loved the forest, had always loved the
forest. He loved the fact that once your ears got used
to the silence you started to hear the endless trees
whispering, then birdsong tuned in. And finally, you
could hear the screech and crackle of wildlife as it
scurried about its tooth-and-claw business. And you
realized that most of what was going on out there
was savage, if mostly silent.

He moved forward slowly. Already, underfoot,
the ground was beginning to soften with its blanket
of leaves and he bent to collect some mushrooms
he spotted that had sprung up there overnight. It
was the perfect time for them and if the hotel had
been as quiet as usual, he'd have happily spent the
rest of the day foraging and dreaming up different

recipes to try in secret.

He was just pocketing a good hoard of mush-rooms when he made out a shadowy figure bent low next to one of the walls. He and Professor Papperspook were not the only people up and about early.

But why was Dr Thallomius's personal assistant out early? And what exactly was she doing?

He was determined not to lose the opportunity to find out.

From her crouched position, Angelique lifted her cane. Seth thought it was pointing directly at him and ducked as she released a dramatic sizzling flash of blue.

But it was the window that got it, a gentle cascade like a waterfall of bright blue light. Seth flinched, expecting the window to shatter, but the glow just flowed around it, turning the glass a glorious shade of forget-me-nots in the frosty morning air.

She wasn't wearing the rustling silk gown of last night, nor the crimson cape. She was wearing a dark suit, a red shirt and shoes that were little suited to crouching in the mud like she was doing now. She was still holding her cane and Seth watched her put away a pencil-thin torch into her red handbag. So Angelique had been out here since before it was light.

The snap of a twig beneath his foot as he moved in for a closer look sounded as loud as a gunshot in the clear, frosty air.

But all she did was remove a notebook from the red handbag she was carrying, frown to herself and jot something down.

Seth breathed a sigh of relief, not quite able to believe that he'd got away with it. As Angelique scribbled more notes, he wondered if he could creep around and get close enough to see what she was writing.

'Make a habit of spying on people do you?' She lifted her sharp, dark eyes and they bored directly into his.

'Erm,' he stammered. 'Well, what are you doing?'

She tucked away her notebook. 'I asked first,' she said, managing to look down her tilted nose even as she rose from her crouched position. 'Out and about bright and early?' She made it sound like an accusation.

'It is the most amazing garden,' he gabbled. 'Whatever you need, you can somehow find it, which is peculiar because of course apples have a different season to strawberries.'

She flipped the silver top of her cane and Seth ducked as she sent a light shower of cornflower-blue sparkles into the icy morning sky. The sparkles held in the frostbitten air for a blinding second and moved to wrap themselves around the wall in front of him.

Seth watched, entranced, as the shimmer of blue crystals hung suspended in the air, just for a second, before melting away. Angelique frowned at the end of her cane.

The walls of the hotel answered with a shuddering sigh.

Angelique snapped shut the top on her cane. 'Show me.'

They fell into step. The sun was rising rapidly, spreading a welcome warm and pink glow behind the dark outlines of trees, making it look like the forest beyond the garden was in flames. Angelique used the cane to help her walk over the uneven ground.

'Are you taking some sort of readings with that cane? Are you . . . are you doing magic?' Seth asked timidly.

Seth hadn't yet worked out if she actually needed it or that was just an excuse for carrying it.

'If you must know, I got bitten on the ankle,' snapped Angelique.

Seth felt himself colour and realized he must have

been staring at her leg, wondering if it was a monster that bit her, or simply someone she'd been snarky to last week.

'Sorry to hear that. So, is your red cane one of those magical inventions?'

'It's a divinoscope. It's very sensitive.'

'Can I look at it?' he asked eagerly.

She pulled it back sharply. 'I said it's very sensitive.'

He felt stung by her snappy attitude, but showed her the way back past the greenhouse, hardly able to believe they were simply walking in this garden, like he had done every day of his life – and they were talking about magic as if it was the most natural thing in the world.

'So what is a divinoscope exactly?'

'It can follow ripples of even very stale magic.'

Seth wanted to know why on earth anyone should want to follow ripples of very stale magic, but instead said, 'What is being magic like? Were you born magic?'

'Magic is complicated.' Angelique gave a shrug of her slim shoulders. 'It's a bit like cooking, Seth.' She said it with a bright smile like she was talking to an idiot. 'Some follow a recipe exactly and it still doesn't work out. Some folk believe it's because you need to be born with a spark of something, some natural ability. And what your magical ability might be varies. But even simple magic can take months of study and practice to perfect. Magic is mostly hard work.'

Hard work. Seth found it difficult to believe magic was anything other than tremendously exciting. 'So this Prospect – Oh, do you mind me asking you all these questions?'

He was rewarded with a huge and weary sigh from Angelique.

She delved into the shiny red handbag she carried everywhere. She pushed something in the flat of her palm right under Seth's nose.

'This might help you.'

'What is it?'

'This is what you get if you do OK at the Prospect. If you prove you have a spark of genuine magic and get accepted into the Elysee. Just for now you can borrow mine.'

Seth peered forward, his heart thundering madly to see what she had taken out of her bag, expecting to see something marvellous, something magical.

It looked like a red credit card, smooth, flat, shiny and rectangular.

'Erm – what exactly is it?'

'This? This is the doorway to magic.'

# 24. A Towering Skyscraper of Books

Seth could only stare as she held the small shiny card in the flat of her hand. He felt distinctly unimpressed.

But as Angelique held out the card, it started to grow. An image twisted and formed and it was like looking into a room in miniature.

'This is the most valuable thing to a sorcerer. However natural your magic, Seth, however good you think you are, no sorcerer should ever stop studying. Magic in the hands of someone who does

no study and does not know what they are doing –
now that definitely is dangerous. This is a library
card.'

'Seriously?' Seth wanted to laugh. 'A library card?
Everyone is putting themselves through the Prospect
for a library card?'

Angelique let out a small tsk of annoyance and
tossed her hair. 'Getting an Elysee library card is a
tremendous honour. A ticket to the secret Elysee
library of magical texts? How can you not be
excited? There is nothing so brilliant and unexpected as the wonders you'll find in a book.'

Seth looked back down at the card. It was growing
again. He could make out a beautiful old room, vast,
seemingly endless, with an arched ceiling, full of
shafts of daylight that highlighted ancient maps and
globes. But what you noticed most was the books.
Shelves and shelves of them, towering upwards, like a
skyscraper of books.

Seth pressed his nose against what Angelique was
showing him. A moving picture. He could almost
have stepped into the room.

Even this early he could see there were people
wandering among the stacks, taking books off
shelves, looking through them and sitting down at
long wooden tables to read. Learning to be magic.

'It's a magical device?' he said in awe. 'Like the sort of thing Dr Thallomius might have invented?'

'Dr Thallomius didn't invent this, but yes, it is magical.'

She used her fingers to walk along a narrow line between two towering stacks and moved her fingers across so Seth's vision focused in on a shelf, then on a book with a green spine, *The Wars of Enlightenment – a brief history of the magical world up to the forty-two deaths in the Unpleasant*. He couldn't resist moving his own finger closer and watched in disbelief as the book removed itself from the shelf, turned so he could see the cover and started to glide towards him, growing in size, getting closer and closer to his finger and bigger and—

She slapped his finger away. The image vanished.

She did something he didn't see, then she put the card back in her handbag. But then she handed him something. It was the book.

He took it in amazement, holding it, taking in the weight of the pages, the rough green of the cover and the smell of paper that told it had just been removed from sitting snugly alongside friends.

It was the very book he had been looking at. But hadn't that just been a picture held in Angelique's hands? 'It feels just like a real book.'

'Yes, Seth. It is a real book. But it's also – oh just go the back page.'

Seth flicked through to the back cover where he exposed a small piece of jagged rock, dark grey, nestled into the binding.

'What's a lump of grey rock doing in a book?' asked Seth, his fingers closing around it.

'Because it's not a lump of grey rock, it's a book with a wordstone in it. It's another magical invention. It makes it easier and quicker to read.'

He lifted the stone. It didn't look the least bit magical. Immediately he touched it, it started to glow like it had been switched on inside.

He felt it turn smooth and flatten, and then the end reshaped itself before his eyes, becoming pointed, then sharp as if you could use it as a weapon or slice through vegetables in no time at all. It turned a lush, vivid emerald green that reminded Seth of ferns.

He stood, marvelling at the glowing green stone in his hand. But then a new sound made him look up. A stomping, as if a colossal elephant was thundering towards them.

Something was coming through the trees in a hurry. Coming straight for them! Seth looked up at the dark forest ahead, shielding his eyes from the low sunlight, and could see the nearby trees were starting to bend and their branches crack. Something huge was lumbering towards them. Something terrible and dangerous.

He looked at Angelique, tried to open his mouth to warn her. The woods were dark and contained many creatures he'd never even seen, but nothing so big, so noisy. And it was getting closer.

There came a roar and a giant head on the end of a long neck poked sideways through the nearest clump of trees, twitching angrily, and a giant malevolent orange eye locked directly on him.

Seth went rigid with terror, unable to even move a muscle, let alone run, as the creature took a slow step forward, clearing the tops of the trees. It stood in the open, just a few feet away, opened its mouth and a long, terrifying jet of fire burst the dry leaves into a line of flaming torches. Next, its head turned towards Seth.

# 25. One of Those Magical Inventions

'Dragon.' Seth found his voice and could only weakly croak.

He tried to clutch at Angelique, but could not take his eyes off the red and gold scales of the monster glinting in the early sunlight. It put its head down, pointing directly at Seth, opened its mouth to reveal two long glistening rows of pointed teeth. Out poured another blast of fire.

He felt something tug at his hand and the dragon disappeared. It had completely vanished. Seth blinked twice.

Angelique stood in front of him waving the word-stone in front of his face. 'It's a brief history of the magical world, Seth. Why are you looking so terrified?'

'Dragon,' he squeaked, lifting his arm to point behind her at the brace of trees where the monstrous creature had been standing only seconds before.

She looked over and sighed. 'It's not a real dragon.' She tossed her hair dismissively. 'Obviously you have gone right back to the beginning. It probably goes way back to ancient times, when people could access the magic that dragons hold. Clearly you can't become magic that way any more.'

'Why not?'

'Um, because dragons were hunted to extinction hundreds of years ago?' She rolled her eyes. 'Even buried in these deep dark woods you must know dragons no longer exist, Seth. Now, try to turn the volume down a bit. Maybe skip that chapter.'

Angelique was giving one of her annoyed frowns, but Seth was finding it easier to put up with her impatience, he was getting used to it.

'You picked this up pretty quickly,' she said, not able to keep the surprise out of her voice as she handed him back the stone. His fingers touched it reluctantly. She was giving him a curious look. 'Most people only get words going into their head when they first use one.'

'How do you turn it down?' he turned it over.

'Don't look for a volume control. You just have to control it with your mind.'

'Like a virtual reality thing?'

'No Seth. It is not a virtual reality thing. It's magic. Think of a question. Think of something you really want an answer to from that book. Try that.'

Seth tentatively gripped the wordstone and tried to do as she suggested and think about what he wanted from it. *Don't think about the dragon.*

But the only thing he could think of was the utter excitement that he was about to do magic. He tried to calm his thoughts.

They had continued walking and had reached the bush where apricots grew in profusion and as Angelique got busy right away, lifting the cane and sending out a shower of sparks over the bush, Seth thought about the Prospect and how his understanding of the magical world was slowly growing.

He knew there was much he didn't yet know, but he also knew he had to understand it if he had any chance of figuring out who had committed the crime and clearing his own name.

Dr Thallomius's changes had led to the Unpleasant. This might be the answer of what had led to one of the people here at the hotel wanting to murder him.

Seth closed his fingers firmly around the stone and closed his eyes.

He sensed something appearing next to his left elbow and he turned. He opened his eyes and found himself looking at a small figure standing right there next to him. He recognized the small figure immediately.

It was Dr Thallomius.

## 26. More Important Than Being Popular

Seth dropped the stone in shock.

The image instantly faded. Angelique this time didn't even turn from where she was examining the shrubbery. 'Dragon back again?'

'N-no, it's Dr Thallomius,' stammered Seth.

He kind of guessed it wasn't real, but it was still difficult to see that image, that cherubic face and not feel both sad and scared.

'Ah yes. Guess he's bound to be in the book. Did you ask a question about him?'

Seth nodded and thought of that wonderful magical library and that towering skyscraper of books. 'So, if Dr Thallomius is in a book – can we talk to him? Ask him who murdered him?'

Angelique let out another deep sigh. 'It's a magical device that makes reading really effortless, Seth. In that book you get a concise history of the magical community, right up to the Unpleasant. But you only get from it what's written in the book.' She gave one of her impatient puffs. 'Thought this was going to be easier than me telling you. Why don't you try again?'

He bent to pick up the stone, holding it loosely in his fingers. This time when he gripped it he was ready as Dr Thallomius came into view. He told himself firmly it was just an image, it wasn't real. It was just a book becoming an image. He gripped the stone.

*The forest was fading, replaced by a small room with big windows where Dr Thallomius went to take a seat at a desk.*

*Seth was watching him from a corner of the room; the trees, the bushes, Angelique, everything had gradually faded until it had vanished and Seth was left staring at Dr Thallomius, who pressed his hands together thoughtfully.*

'What our dwindling magical world desperately needs is young, fresh, enthusiastic people, who are eager to train and will work hard,' said Dr Thallomius.

Dr Thallomius didn't seem aware of Seth at all. He was frowning over a large document, gripping a shiny purple pen and hesitating, glancing towards something to Seth's right.

'Everyone knows it, but no one has the courage to do it.' Where was that twinkle in his eye? He looked a lot more serious. 'I mean to start a recruitment drive.'

'You don't mean to have an open invitation to join the Elysee?'

The voice to Seth's right made him jump. Someone he couldn't even see, but he thought he recognized the voice of Count Marred.

'That is exactly it!' said Dr Thallomius. 'Magical people used to be everywhere. Magical folk are becoming so rare that people are starting to forget we even exist. People don't even believe in magic any more.' Dr Thallomius shook his head sadly. 'We have to act. If we don't scour the country and find the best and most promising new recruits – where will it end? We need keen and talented novices and fresh blood. We need to root out anyone who has just a sprinkle of real magic and make sure it is nurtured in the right direction.'

He looked like he was waiting for a comment and

*eventually the other voice replied.*

*'You might just make an enemy of some of the most influential magical families.'*

Dr Thallomius gave a hollow chuckle and picked up the pen, but his hand still hesitated over thick sheets of paper. *'I know what I'm proposing might upset people. But with a real danger of magic dying out completely, what choice do we have? Someone must have the courage to act. But what I mean to propose – well, at least no one will be able to accuse us and say how we recruit isn't fair. Everyone must be given an equal chance.'*

*'I don't understand. What exactly do you mean to do?'*

Dr Thallomius got to his feet and started pacing the small office, his hands behind his back, his head jutting forward. Seth stepped back, fearing he'd lose the image if he collided with it.

*'We need to change the rules of entry for the Elysee. It should be for anyone with a real flair for magic and the dedication to succeed – those are the ones who should be given the chance, whatever their background. It is too flawed to simply rely on magic being passed to children. Magic is much more complicated than that. Magic is drawn to where it wants to go.'*

*'If I have understood correctly, what you are proposing... This is going to be ... unpopular.'*

'I propose a procedure where all are given a chance to demonstrate suitability to join the magical world. Everyone will be judged by the same rules and everyone will be asked to undergo it. Only those who pass will be invited to be officially part of our magical community. It'll be called the Prospect.'

There was a short silence. 'You mean to make everyone go through this Prospect? Even those who feel a place is rightfully theirs? Even those who have been long-standing members of the magical community?' the voice said quietly. 'You'll have such opposition. That could even be dangerous.'

'Luckily, saving the magical world is more important to me than being popular.' Dr Thallomius stopped and looked towards the voice who had given the warning.

He thumped his hand down on the pile of paper. Golden sparks showered from his hands and he brushed away black speckles of ashes from the top sheet.

'We must stop the Elysee being a private club for magical families. Magic is dying. There is no other way. It's the Prospect – or it's the end of magic.' He slammed his fist on the desk again.

'It is the bravest policy I have heard of in a generation.'

Dr Thallomius gave a grim smile, returned to his seat, picked up the pen and signed his name with a flourish. 'Thank you – I think. I'm sure everyone will *come around to seeing that it's for the best. I feel sure everything will be absolutely fine.'*

The image faded. Seth slid the stone into one of his pockets and it took a moment to take in the familiar trees. And Angelique standing there waiting.

'Dr Thallomius made things tough for himself, didn't he? Is that why people like Red Valerian are against him? It isn't even so much that he started this apprentice scheme looking for new recruits, it's more that he's making old magical families prove their worth?'

Angelique looked at him for such a long time it made him feel uncomfortable. 'Our Sorcerer General was a brave man.'

'He didn't realize just how angry some magical folk would be, did he?'

Angelique turned and headed back towards the hotel and Seth followed, feeling even sadder than ever that Dr Thallomius, with all his brave and fair policies, had died.

They walked in silence, then Seth spotted some green leaves, tiny, with distinctive serrated edges. It was a herb he had been looking out for and was exactly what he needed. He dived off the path and knelt to pick some. He took out one of the leather pouches he carried everywhere in his pockets to place the leaves inside.

'Do you do this a lot?'

'Err, yes,' replied Seth, feeling Angelique's steady gaze. 'Haven't seen these for a while and I use them to make a special tea for Henri. Helps with his indigestion. Did you find what you were looking for? With your divinoscope?'

'When you say you can find anything growing in the garden, could you find Wolfbane?'

Seth thought back to the many herbs his father had taught him about. 'That's not a medicinal herb. Isn't that rather dangerous?' Once again, all his senses seemed to be reminding him not to trust Angelique.

She had still completely avoided telling him what she was up to with that cane of hers. She had told him it followed ripples of even very stale magic, but how was he supposed to even know what she meant?

'Only in the wrong hands, Seth. So could you get some?'

'Probably.'

'And what about figwort?

'If I wanted to, although you shouldn't really—'

'And squill – not too much, just a pinch. How long would it take to get all those together?'

'I couldn't say exactly. What do you want them for?'

Her dark eyes avoided meeting his.

'Can I keep the book?' he asked.

Angelique hesitated. 'Oh I suppose so. Only it's on my library card so don't get it back late or lose it, don't damage it, don't do anything to it, OK?'

'But I can read it? And if I get you those herbs, will you tell me what you are doing with your divinoscope? As long as you're not planning to use those herbs for anything bad.'

'Bad, Seth? Me?' she wrinkled her nose. 'What on earth do you mean?' Then Angelique took a quick glance around her. They were almost back at the hotel. 'Seth, I need to talk to you. You remember me saying you might be the only person who can help me?'

'Because I've lived here so long?'

She nodded. 'I am sure you have all the answers.'

She gave him such a long and penetrating look with those intelligent brown eyes of hers. For an uncomfortable moment he felt as if she knew all about the black book.

'I really know nothing.'

'Well, if you promise not to tell anyone what I am about to tell you – and I mean no one, it's crucial – then I will tell you what I've been doing, or trying to do. Because there is so much here I don't understand.

And you can help me, Seth. In fact, you must.'

'OK, OK, I get it. You can trust me, Angelique.'

He wished he could trust her.

'I've been taking readings. About magic.'

Seth could only look at her blankly.

'Specifically whether magic has been used recently. It leaves a mark in the air. To most people it would be completely invisible. But there are ripples.' Angelique moved the dramatic stripe of red in her dark hair to behind her ear. 'Seth, the first time we spoke you said you'd never heard of magic.'

'I know.'

'But Seth,' Angelique took another reading from the end of her cane and looked about her, 'there is magic everywhere here.'

Seth stopped completely and could only look at her, wide-eyed. 'But there are magical people here – they are here for the Prospect?'

'That's not what I mean. That does not fit with what my readings are telling me.'

'That's what your divinoscope is telling you? It must be faulty.'

Angelique drew herself up, insulted. 'Faulty? It is not faulty. You have to help me Seth, because something is not right. The magic here, it's not stale magic. It's magic I don't really . . .' Angelique chewed her lip and carried on, she was talking mostly to herself. 'It's distorted magic. That's the only way I can describe it. It's like at this hotel someone is using a form of magic I've never come across before.'

## 27. Some News on Our Candidates

Some sort of magic? Here? Seth felt his heart skip faster. How could she possibly be right?

He had no chance to collect his thoughts or ask anything more as he caught the smell of fresh coffee arriving on the morning breeze, just ahead of Inspector Pewter looking as fresh and smart as if he'd arrived straight from having his suit pressed and his hair tidied. He was carrying a tray loaded with cups.

'I bring coffee and bad news,' called Pewter,

putting the tray on one of the long tables on the patio outside the hotel lounge.

'Oh no,' said Angelique, covering her mouth with her hand, her eyes widening. 'Someone else hasn't . . . ?'

'I'm sorry to say I appear to have eaten all the shortbread last night. Now there is nothing like a bright and breezy morning to make you want to get started on work right away. And a biscuit always helps. At least, it would do.'

'I'll go and make some more.' Seth went to slip past him, feeling his stomach twist as he realized just how behind he must already be with his many kitchen tasks.

Pewter laid a steadying hand on his arm. 'Today, Mr Seppi, I request that you work with me. Even if we will have to bravely survive without biscuits.'

Seth had been going to suggest that they all go and sit more comfortably inside, rather than out here on a damp, chilly morning. There was still frost everywhere the sun had not yet touched and they only ever used this long table on the patio at the height of summer.

But as he took a seat, it was warm. He even felt a soft summer breeze flutter on his cheek and he looked at Pewter. Was he making it warm here? Was he using magic?

'You, Seth,' began Pewter, 'caused me to get almost no sleep. It was the fault of that supremely impressive question you asked last night.'

'Sorry about that, sir.'

'Miss Squerr!'

Angelique had already started to turn back to the garden.

'Perhaps just for a moment we can forget that you are a suspect here? I would be supremely grateful.'

She flashed him an annoyed look. 'Think I can cope with that. You want something from me. What exactly?' Her dark eyes narrowed.

'You said yesterday you had notes on everyone's magical demonstrations. I would be most interested to know exactly what everyone's skill was that they showed at the Prospect feast.'

Pewter poured them each a cup of coffee. He slid one towards Angelique invitingly. She stared at it, hesitating for a couple of moments before taking a seat that was still damp from the morning dew.

Seth saw Nightshade return from hunting for her breakfast and slip under the table. She was ready to listen, ready to learn; he was doing the same.

Seth searched his mind for anything supremely impressive he had said yesterday. But his mind was too distracted by what Angelique had revealed.

Surely Dr Thallomius's murderer had to be someone from the magical world – someone who had arrived here as a guest to take part in the Prospect?

How could there be magic already here at the hotel?

But then how often had he thought to himself that the garden was magical? Of course he'd never actually believed . . .

'The question you asked, Seth – was this crime committed using magic?' said Pewter, interrupting Seth's thoughts. 'It was almost exactly the question I was asking myself. Because otherwise, it seems an impossible crime. And really, there is no such thing.'

Angelique sipped her coffee. She gave her head a little thoughtful shake. 'But someone getting into that locked room during the only five minutes when it could have been done? That would require seriously impressive magic.'

There was the slamming of a door and Kingfisher stomped out, stroking his moustache, smoothing his green suit and complaining. 'Why is he not under lock and key?' He glared at Seth and Angelique. 'And why is she drinking coffee?'

'I am pleased to say you are not too late for a cup,' replied Pewter.

Kingfisher still glared, but he sat down and accepted the coffee.

'Now, we were just agreeing that we are putting aside all our differences. A time for pooling resources. First, I want to go over one or two details.'

Kingfisher groaned and put his head in his hands.

'Now Miss Squerr was sitting right next to the dessert, which had arrived at the very last second?'

They all nodded.

'After the main course everyone had the chance to show their magic,' said Angelique. 'I did not move the whole time. I made notes and, I'm sorry, but absolutely no one went past me or near that table. Then it was time for dessert and—'

'Who handed Dr Thallomius the dessert?' enquired Pewter.

Seth noticed that Angelique's throat quivered slightly as she whispered. 'That, I'm afraid, was me.' She shook back her hair and rattled her long red fingernails on the table. 'Gregorian,' she said clearly, 'after the food arrived, the dining room was officially sealed ready for the Prospect and was then left empty for five minutes. Can I just check whether we can rule out that that's when the poison was administered? Was the dining room door simply locked or was it charmed for magical intervention? How difficult would it have been to get past?'

'Of course it was charmed. Think I'd forget the

absolute basics?' Kingfisher's lip curled at Angelique thinking she had the right to question him. 'That room was sealed.'

'Did the charms you put in place cover the whole room?' pressed Angelique.

Kingfisher hesitated. 'All right, no,' he snarled. 'I just made sure someone couldn't use an unlocking fix on the door. Myself and Mr Bunn had keys to the two locks. We were all going to be back in five minutes. It's just part of the procedure. It's to keep any evidence that people might be bringing to the Prospect away from the prying eyes of any non-magical people who might be hanging about. Some magical folk are very secretive about their magic, or being magic at all. The charm was definitely still in place when myself and Mr Bunn opened the door again.'

Pewter gave a discreet cough. 'I say let's forget the fact that Thallomius was a political figure with powerful enemies.'

'Forget it?' echoed Kingfisher with a hollow laugh. 'I try to forget politics as often as I can.'

'I agree that focusing on how the crime could have been committed is a good place to start,' said Angelique.

'But we know it can only have been done by the

kitchen boy!'

A rustling behind them and a familiar terrifying smell of ironed sheets and rum warned Seth that his horrible boss Norrie Bunn was approaching and he was about to pay for a fatal mistake. For the first time in his life, he'd completely neglected his duties.

He tried to scramble out of his chair, but not quickly enough. Norrie held the back of it like a steel trap, but her voice, when she spoke to the guests, was syrupy.

'I can only apologize for Seth's manners. He is not well-trained and recent events have upset him. But he should know his place is not to slouch about with the guests.'

Seth felt her bony fingers gripping the back of his chair and she hauled it backwards, nearly sending him flying.

'What on earth are you playing at, boy?' thundered Norrie Bunn, breathing rum fumes right in his face. 'Think guests want to sit about with the kitchen boy?' She turned to give a polite, tight smile to the others.

Seth again tried to get to his feet, but stumbled awkwardly.

'My dear Mrs Bunn, any chance of some more coffee?' Pewter asked politely, waving the empty coffee pot.

Norrie Bunn whipped her head around to look hard at him. 'I shall get Seth on to it right away. That – and the fact that we will soon have hungry guests wanting their breakfast and my kitchen boy hasn't set foot about his duties since yesterday. We are a little behind.'

She now had Seth's wrist gripped so hard he thought his bones would crack.

'That does seem very troublesome, Mrs Bunn,' said Pewter smoothly. 'I can see why you are so keen to get young Seth back into your kitchen.'

Norrie started to drag Seth away.

'I am impressed by the way you so easily cope with having a notorious poisoner among your kitchen staff.'

Mrs Bunn loosened her grip on Seth as if he'd set his hand on fire. She looked at him in horror and turned to Pewter, a look of slow uncertainty crossing her sharp features.

Pewter checked the enormous watch on his wrist.

'Are you certain Seth poisoned one of my guests?' Norrie hissed. 'I heard that yesterday you were trying to pin it on my daughter.'

'Rest assured, investigations are proceeding, but currently we have absolutely no reason to suspect anyone else.'

'I really should go and help in the kitchen,' said Seth.

Pewter gave his head a very small shake and frowned. He turned to Kingfisher. 'I guess someone could offer some help?'

Kingfisher looked aghast, pointing a finger to his chest. 'Me?'

'Well that's very kind of you to offer – Mrs Bunn, Mr Fishfinger will come and assist you. Shall we say five minutes?'

Seth couldn't believe it when Mrs Bunn simply scuttled off. He sat down again, although Angelique turned to him with a smile that only made him dread what was coming.

'Seth's been an eager student about the magical world. Now's a good time to show that you've been paying attention.'

Seth felt his face go hot as everyone turned to him, waiting.

'Erm.' Seth cleared his throat. 'Well. Magic is rare. It is difficult to do. It can be dark and dangerous. It's a responsibility, because there are different kinds of magic and some of them are . . . horrible. And it can take ages to learn to do even basic stuff. That's probably why there aren't that many magical people about, I guess.' He scratched his head.

'That's pretty good Seth, glad to see you really have been paying attention,' said Angelique.

Seth turned to Pewter. 'When you said I almost asked the same question as you were asking yourself, you weren't thinking about whether it was committed by magic. I guess what you were already thinking is – who here could have had enough magic to have done it?'

Pewter beamed. 'My thoughts exactly. Which is why I am involving you, Miss Squerr.' He rubbed his hands. 'We proceed. Miss Squerr, you took notes. And I remember you saying Dr Thallomius came all this way to judge a huddle of not-very-promising hopefuls. So ... some news on our candidates, please. Let's see what we make of them.'

Angelique didn't speak straight away. She tapped a smart red pen on the table top. 'You think one of them is deceiving us? Hiding more magical ability than they want to reveal? You think someone might have tricked their way into this Prospect? That someone who secretly has strong magical powers is hiding behind being a novice?'

'I say we run with it as a possibility. You could even call it the perfect crime,' said Pewter. 'But luckily I like a challenge.'

## 28. ANOTHER WAY?

Angelique took out her red notebook and flipped it open. 'Count Marred was pitching a simple wellbeing potion. A few small glasses of his colourless fluid he calls Broom and you get a warm glow of happiness and start to feel that everyone around you is your friend.'

'Sounds fantastic,' said Pewter. 'That'll be popular. I'd have some of that.'

The fact that Count Marred had demonstrated his ability to brew a potion made Seth sit up. That sounded promising.

'Hmm,' went on Angelique. 'I would say a hint of magical ability. But it is so incredibly difficult to judge.' She sighed. 'Dr Thallomius was so good at that.'

'Professor Papperspook – expert on birds, particularly an ability to talk to them,' sneered Kingfisher, swinging on his chair. 'I don't think you're going to eliminate suspects that way. Seth, for instance, isn't magic in the slightest.' He gave Seth the most unfriendly smile ever.

Seth fidgeted, trying to change the subject. 'I think Mr Bunn used to keep birds. He keeps a tiny bird cage, which is strange when he has a very strict "no pets" rule. I helped Professor Papperspook collect some bird song this morning. It was fascinating.'

Kingfisher gave him a long, searching look, before turning back to Pewter and growling. 'I guess Troutbean was a wash-out?'

'But wasn't her grandfather a famous sorcerer?' asked Seth.

Angelique pulled a face. 'Miss Troutbean claims to have invented an anti-gravity dust, but that was always going to be pretty unlikely.'

'Why's that?' asked Seth.

'Anti-gravity dust? That would be Tier One wizardry. If Miss Troutbean had developed that level of magic at her age it would be incredible. Magic takes study and hard work to perfect, you just said you understood that,' said Angelique.

'You mean even people born into magical families try to trick their way into the Elysee?'

Angelique gave a small nod. 'I'm afraid magic being inherited from your parents is never guaranteed.'

'In Miss Troutbean's case she's pretty angry at the fact any magic in that family seems to have skipped her completely,' drawled Kingfisher.

'But how was she making it look like she'd invented an anti-gravity dust?' pressed Seth.

'Miss Troutbean had springs in her shoes. Pretty easy to spot.'

Seth remembered those peculiar thick-soled shoes he'd found when he'd searched Gloria's room.

From having a glimmer of hope that they would be able to find the answer, Seth was back to wracking his brains again. It was beginning to look like none of the guests had enough magical ability to have done it. How was it done?

'Miss Squerr, you have been most enlightening,' said Pewter. 'Seth, I hope you haven't forgotten that you asked me another extremely good question and Miss Squerr, I believe, is about to tell us the answer – who was this mysterious eighth person at the Prospect table last night?'

## 29. THE EiGHTH SEAT

Anoise from the shrubbery distracted them all. Seth could think of one person who was supremely good at creeping around, listening in and looking for a chance to get him into trouble.

He looked up and wondered if he should tell them Tiffany could very well be lurking, but after a few seconds everything went quiet. It was probably just a bird. Angelique pressed on and her words caught Seth completely by surprise.

'The eighth seat at the table was not for a guest.

Someone invited us to have our Prospect meeting here and be judged on an application to join the Elysee.'

It sank in what she was saying. 'What? Someone here at the hotel wanted to demonstrate magic? Someone here applied to join the magical world? Who? Who was it?' demanded Seth.

'Horatio Bunn.'

'Mr Bunn? Mr Bunn thinks he is magical?'

So that was why Mr Bunn had been so very excited – he was actually going to the dinner. That was why all the magical folk ended up coming here to the Last Chance Hotel. And that explained why Mr Bunn had been the first one to call for help when Dr Thallomius was poisoned. Mr Bunn had been first on the scene because he had been inside the room all the time.

More rustling in the nearby shrubbery made them all turn. This time it was unmistakeable and King-fisher went reluctantly to investigate, although he returned quickly, shaking his head.

Angelique consulted the notebook again. 'I'd like your opinion, Seth. On your master. Mr Bunn.'

Seth could give plenty of opinions about Mr Bunn, but he had a feeling she wasn't interested in how mean and lazy he was.

'He had something pretty amazing to show us,' said Angelique, shuffling her papers.

Seth was listening in growing disbelief. Surely Mr Bunn would simply be another fraudster, hoping he could trick his way into the Elysee, get a library card and access to all those wonderful magical books and train to be magic? Surely Mr Bunn had only found a way to do an impressive trick.

'What did he do?' Seth demanded.

'He did magic with two carved figures of bugs.'

'Henri's,' muttered Seth. 'He spends his free time carving those. What magic did Mr Bunn do with the carvings?'

'He did something very few people would ever have the skill to do.' She twirled the long strand of red in her hair around her index finger. 'Something incredible.' Angelique consulted her notes carefully before speaking and the frown deepened. 'I don't know how he did it. If it was a trick it was an extremely good one. It certainly looked like proper magic.'

'What did he do to Henri's animals?'

He expected her to say he smashed them up, or burnt them. He imagined something dramatic to seize the attention.

'If there was anyone in that room who performed

magic impressive enough to make me think he could have got past those charms Kingfisher put on the door just before the Prospect, it would be your boss.'

Seth could bear it no longer. 'What exactly did he do?'

'Personification. He made those little carved figures move. He made them come to life.'

# 30. A GRUDGE AGAINST WINTERGREEN

Professor Papperspook emerged from the lounge door and two steps behind her shuffled the reluctant Gloria, twisting the sleeve of her cardigan.

'Ah, delightful of you to join us, Professor, can I offer you coffee?'

'How long are you keeping us here?' she demanded.

'Or are you more of a tea drinker?' said Pewter. 'And please accept my profuse apologies for the lack of biscuits. I take personal responsibility for that.' He passed her a coffee anyway.

Professor Papperspook puffed up her chest, but accepted the cup. 'You can't keep us here.'

'I rather think that as a murder has been committed we can,' muttered Pewter.

Seth was hardly listening. How on earth had Mr Bunn done magic?

The professor steamrollered on. 'Are we all under suspicion?' She didn't wait for an answer. 'Then I hope you have looked seriously at that the miniature entertainer who calls himself a magician. When the rest of us went to get changed after that game of cards, he followed Dr Thallomius straight to his room. I heard them arguing.'

'Arguing?' said Kingfisher uncertainly. 'What about?'

'I'd imagine they had plenty to argue about. He's exactly the sort of chancer out to defraud the magical community that the Elysee doors have been opened to, all thanks to Dr Thallomius and this ridiculous recruitment drive of his.'

'You are not a supporter of the changes Dr Thallomius has been bringing to the Elysee?' Angelique closed her red notebook with a snap.

'Magic belongs in magical hands,' said Papperspook, puffing herself up, her clothes billowing around her as if she was resetting her feathers.

'Littering the magical community with untrained upstarts. Torpor Thallomius had quite different views when he was young. He could not have been closer with Wintergreen Troutbean, getting up to no end of high jinks those two – inventing that famous burglar alarm that inflated people by a few centimetres so they couldn't escape the way they had come in. So are you investigating that upstart boy properly? He could easily have slipped poison into that glass, that's exactly the sort of trick he excels at. Hoping we'll rule him out because he is young and so very short.'

'With poison,' drawled Kingfisher, 'age and size hardly comes into it.'

Professor Papperspook drew herself up to her full height, which made her complicated and colourful hair start to nod. 'Are you suggesting my niece—'

Seth decided it was a good time to head for the kitchen and slipped away, hearing Pewter saying something like they must all be hungry and suggesting that they move to the comfortable hotel lounge while they awaited the call for breakfast.

Was Mr Bunn out to defraud the Elysee into awarding him a place? Or could he really do magic? There was only one way to find out more.

He had to find Mr Bunn and not let him out of

his sight. He simply had to discover what his boss was up to.

Breakfast could not have been further from Seth's mind, so he sneaked up to the door to the kitchen and listened.

'It's only scrambling eggs, sweet pea,' Norrie was saying. 'You can scramble an egg.'

'Why can't Dad and Henri help?' Tiffany moaned.

'The question is where is that boy! Only thinking of himself. Where has he got to? Under arrest for murder. If you ask me, it's just an excuse to get him out of doing his jobs.'

There was a smell of burning.

'Even Seth could manage to scramble an egg, sweet pea.' Norrie sounded cross. 'Just what exactly are you learning at that expensive school of yours?'

Seth fled before Norrie Bunn could discover him lurking in the doorway and put him to work. So Mr Bunn wasn't in the kitchen. Then where was he? What was Mr Bunn up to?

Seth darted a quick look in the lounge, where the guests were assembling. He could hear them all trying hard to be polite to each other. But no Mr Bunn.

He made a quiet dash to his attic room. Nightshade was stretched out full length on the bed like a puddle of darkness, catching up with some snooze time.

Angeliquc had told him there was magic here at the hotel, some sort of distorted magic. How had Mr Bunn managed to do magic?

Seth sank on to the end of the bed, wondering, and earning a sharp reproving claw in the leg.

'I'm not asleep. I'm on the case,' Nightshade muttered drowsily.

Seth stroked her soft fur.

He thought of Angelique jetting everything with a fierce blue light. He thought how the walls of the hotel had seemed to respond with a threatening rumble.

'Just leave the breakfast in the bowl as usual,' muttered Nightshade.

Seth slowly reached out, extending his arm towards the longest wall in the room, slowly lengthening his fingers, reaching tentatively towards the rough cracked plaster of his attic room. Was it possible there could be magic here? Actually in the walls?

He flexed his fingers nervously, not daring to even brush the wall, as if just touching it might bring that voice again.

'Do stop wriggling,' snapped Nightshade, giving

him another jab in the leg.

Seth brought his fingers back in sharply.

'You're getting distracted, Seth. Kingfisher still wants to arrest you. He's the one you've got to convince. You've got to get something on one of the others. They all seem to have a reason to want Dr Thallomius out of the picture. Which of them is it, Seth?'

He stroked Nightshade. 'What about Mr Bunn?'

'Old Bunn? I was under the table. I heard all about him doing magic. Is that your best idea?'

'It really sounds like he did magic.'

Seth took out his black book and flicked again through the pages. His eyes alighted on the image of what looked like a lantern or tiny birdcage with beautiful shafts of intense light zinging out of the device. The firefly cage. He had thought it beautiful, but after Angelique telling him he didn't even want to know what it did, the picture now looked strange and frightening. Why was that picture in this book?

'So how did he do it?'

The only reply Nightshade gave was a little contended snickering purr that sounded exactly like a snore.

'Sometimes I really do feel the answers are so close I could reach out and touch them,' said Seth, giving her a nudge. 'Nightshade? I need to ask you a favour. If Norrie catches sight of me I'll lose any chance to keep an eye on Mr Bunn.' He dropped the book absent-mindedly on the bed, his mind busy with possibilities. 'You could easily keep an eye on Mr Bunn and he won't notice you. Find out if you can spot him doing any magic.'

'Keep an eye on Mr Bunn doing magic,' muttered Nightshade sleepily. 'On it.'

Even if Mr Bunn really had done magic at the Prospect, that still did not answer the question of how the poison had got into that dessert. Seth headed back to search for Mr Bunn, his mind whirring. He still had a long way to go.

# 31. AN EXPLOSIVE COMBINATION

But before Seth could even begin his plan to keep an eye on Mr Bunn, it wasn't Norrie who dragged him off to do something else. He was accosted by Inspector Pewter and led to what had been Dr Thallomius's room. The door creaked open, revealing a room that felt flat; silent and untouched from when Dr Thallomius had pressed that gold coin into Seth's palm.

He remembered the kindness of Dr Thallomius as he'd stood there only yesterday and Seth felt a lump rise in his throat.

That faint smell of grassy tea lingered. The two tea cups were still on the small polished side table where the two old friends had chatted.

Pewter dug around in his pocket and extracted an enormous magnifying glass and turned to examine the door.

'Are you checking for fingerprints?' Seth asked as Pewter next crossed to the big, curved four-poster bed. Alongside it was Dr Thallomius's suitcase, neatly closed.

'Ah, fingerprints,' Pewter shook his head. 'Have heard of that. Sounds very clever. A trifle messy I suspect.'

Seth went across and sniffed deeply at the dregs left in the cups, looking for that unforgettable pungent smell in the dining room as Dr Thallomius lay dead. But that smell was nowhere in this room. His nose told him there was simply tea in one of the cups, and the other contained some sort of herb, spearmint, probably.

Pewter had gone to lie full length on the bed. He was over six feet tall and even in the enormous bed his feet dangled off the end; he was flicking through the book left on the bedside table.

Seth expected a magical text borrowed from the

Elysee library, but it was an Agatha Christie mystery, the sort Norrie Bunn read and sometimes passed on to Seth. *The Mysterious Affair at Styles.* The sort of story where someone was murdered and everyone started to look at each other and wonder who might be next.

'You said you needed my help?'

'Indeed I do. We are looking for clues,' said Pewter. 'Specifically, we are hoping that Dr Thallomius left us a clue to what he was really doing here.'

'Wasn't he judging the Prospect?'

'That's what he said he was here for,' said Pewter. 'But people don't always tell the truth, do they?'

Pewter peered at Seth, who tried hard not to look back guiltily. He wanted to ask all sorts of things, like what Pewter thought of Mr Bunn doing magic. But it was difficult without giving away things that were supposed to be secret, like mentioning about Angelique and the walls talking. She had told him it was top secret that she was investigating magic at the hotel with her divinoscope.

'You seem pretty friendly with Miss Squerr,' said Pewter, interrupting Seth's thoughts and leaving him with the uncomfortable idea that somehow he had known Seth had been thinking about Angelique. 'Has she confided in you as to what she's really doing here?'

'Really doing here?' Seth thoughts flew to Angelique and that cane of hers. What had she told him? Something he didn't understand about ripples. Then she had made him promise not to breathe a word, and told him she had found magic here at the hotel. But she hadn't explained anything, had she? And it was very strange behaviour for Dr Thallomius's assistant. Why had she been looking for magic? And what had that meant about it being magic she had never seen before?

Seth looked into Pewter's light-blue eyes and felt himself swallow quietly and knew he was still under suspicion. He watched his eyes glow a darker blue, as if Pewter could read his every thought, everything he was anxious to conceal. Angelique dashing about with her cane, sending out the blue sparks and getting him to promise silence. She had nearly zapped him too when he'd let slip he'd heard of a firefly cage. He must not let on about knowing of sinister magical devices.

'Believe everything she tells you, do you?' went on Pewter pleasantly. 'Trust her do you?'

Seth thought for a moment.

Then remembered he didn't trust her at all.

He had probably given himself away by being silent for so long. Pewter was looking at him, his eyes glinting like pieces of sky through a high window.

'She told me about Red Valerian, sir. If he's a known enemy of Dr Thallomius, can't you arrest him?'

'Told you that, did she? Yes, pulling him in would be a great plan. Red Valerian is someone who has been giving MagiCon headaches. Actually, less a headache and more organizing his followers in arranging most unpleasant deaths.' Pewter gazed at him for an uncomfortable few seconds. 'But there is one big obstacle to us bringing him in. We don't have a clue who he is. Some people don't even believe he is a real person – just a name to frighten the children, as it were.'

Pewter crouched next to Dr Thallomius's suitcase, unclipped the clasps and gently went through it.

'I'm impressed with how well you are learning your magical history, Seth. I am interested in your thoughts.'

'My thoughts?' Seth thought hard of something, anything that might sound helpful. 'Dr Thallomius's policies – they led to some sort of battle, called the Unpleasant, right? Because of that, forty-two sorcerers are now Missing Feared Exploded?'

'Indeed, that is sadly true.'

Seth watched Pewter lift up a picture of a pug dog to look behind it. Not for the first time, he wondered if Pewter was really any good as a detective. He itched to be away, watching Mr Bunn, not here, looking for clues that only Pewter seemed to believe existed.

'Dr Thallomius was seeking out people worthy of being apprentices,' went on Seth carefully. 'But also making everyone go through the Prospect, even those from magical families who feel they have a right to be part of the Elysee? He had enemies.'

'You are quite right; some people have been heard to comment that under Thallomius the magical world has become open to every crackpot who ever managed to bend a spoon. We are in a dark period in the world of sorcerers. Now, you were helping me search.'

Seth looked about him.

'The trouble is, sir, that there aren't that many places to hide things in a hotel room.'

'The trouble is,' said Pewter, lifting pillows and peering under the bed, 'that someone has been in here since I searched last night after everyone went to bed.'

Seth stared around him, then at Pewter.

'We can only hope they weren't any more success-ful than me in finding it,' said Pewter. 'All right, Seth. Now, I am relying on you. What have I missed?'

Seth looked about again, not knowing where to begin – the room looked completely untouched. 'Erm – how exactly are you so sure someone has been in here?'

'That'll be the charms I placed after I searched late last night.' He took out his magnifying glass to peer at the carpet. 'But someone got past it all.'

'How can you know that?'

'Fingerprints are beyond me, but you must let me have my own little methods.'

Pewter was looking again through what Seth had taken to be a magnifying glass, but as Seth watched, he doubted it was actually magnifying anything. Pewter, he guessed, was using it for something else.

'Is that another magical device, like the sort of thing Dr Thallomius liked to invent?' he asked.

'Magical this may be, but it still can't tell me who is doing this,' said Pewter, his voice rising and sounding unexpectedly cross. 'Now, what we have here is evidence that someone is finding a very clever way to get past magical charms. Someone is moving about this hotel quite freely, doing what they want and getting into places they are very much not supposed to be. And if there is one thing I hate it is my opponent being one step ahead of me. We need to find what they were looking for before they get to it.'

Seth had watched him go through everything from the bed to the suitcase, even peering behind the pictures. What could he possibly find? What could he possibly be looking for?

Seth concentrated on trying to imagine himself as Dr Thallomius, here in this room. If Pewter was right, he had something he urgently needed to hide. If it was still missing, that meant it had to be something small. Where might it be?

'You haven't tried the top of the wardrobe, sir.'

'Actually, I have.'

'But this one has like a groove that runs around the top. I know because I dust in here. Things get stuck in there.'

Pewter leapt forward and Seth watched him feel methodically from one side to the other, reaching further, stretching his arms then stopping to give a cry of 'Ah!'

Seth could see that, finally, his fingers had struck something. An object small enough to be concealed in his closed hand.

Seth inched his head forward, so that his nose almost touched Pewter's palm. Pewter opened his fist and they both stared at a small object, pale, short, thin and slightly knobbly and a little bit scratched, lying in the palm of his hand.

Was this it?

'It looks like the bone of . . . a small creature.' Seth didn't like to say that the first thought that had flashed into his mind was that it was the bone from a baby's finger.

'Is this usually here?' Pewter asked Seth.

Seth shook his head. 'Absolutely not. I do the cleaning and Norrie Bunn makes sure I do it to her high standards. But with our VIP guest she was fanatical, everything was dusted twice, even the tops of the doors. This definitely was not here before Dr Thallomius arrived. He must have put it there himself. But what is it? Is it important?' It couldn't have looked less important.

'This must be it,' said Pewter. 'What Dr Thallomius hid. What someone else has been searching for.'

'This?'

'It's what really brought Dr Thallomius to the Last Chance Hotel.'

They stared at the tiny, pale, twig-like object. As Seth looked closely he began to think that the scratches might actually be symbols and insignia carefully carved on to the surface. But that didn't help in knowing what it was.

Pewter cleared his throat.

'I think it might be a key.'

'A key sir?'

Pewter was lost in his own thoughts. 'That means Dr Thallomius's real purpose in coming here was to lock something. Or maybe unlock . . .' Pewter scratched his left ear. 'Any ideas, Seth?'

Before Seth could reply, the air was split by an ear-piercing scream.

## 32. The Spectre in the Bedroom

Seth and Pewter thundered towards the source of the scream and were just ahead of Darinder Dunster-Dunstable and Count Marred who were neck and neck when they reached the first-floor landing. They all arrived at Gloria Troutbean's room, where Professor Papperspook was busy trying to calm her.

'Astounding news,' declared Professor Papperspook in a deep and hushed voice. 'We are privileged to have had a communication from Dr Thallomius.'

'What do you mean?' demanded Count Marred.

'Communication?' Kingfisher shoved his way to the front. 'He wrote to you? Something about why he was murdered? Show it to me. Show me the letter.'

Professor Papperspook flapped her hands and waggled them above her head. 'Not that sort of communication.' She moved aside and prodded the timid Gloria forward with her elbow. 'Tell him, Gloria.'

Gloria pulled up her white socks and stood up straight as everyone crowded into her bedroom. 'A communication from him since he departed,' she announced, sounding surprisingly proud, her moon-like face taking on a flush of colour. 'I saw a shadowy figure in the corner of my room.'

'Hang on a minute,' said Kingfisher, his eyes narrowing. 'This important communication was from a ghost?'

'He must be a wandering troubled spirit,' said the Professor, shaking her head sorrowfully.

'It's not him that's troubled,' muttered Kingfisher.

Gloria Troutbean drew herself up fiercely. 'There was a presence in my room. A spectre, I saw it.' Gloria's face took on a blush of ugly crimson.

'And it spoke to you?' said Kingfisher with heavy scepticism.

There was a pause before Gloria said, 'Not exactly.'

'How can you be sure it was Dr Thallomius?' Angelique asked, arriving from somewhere. 'Did you see him clearly?'

'Well do you know of any other troubled spirits lurking around here?' pointed out Papperspook.

'So this apparition – did it say anything?' said Kingfisher, with another sneer.

Professor Papperspook's plumage bristled. 'He has come through to Gloria. We should try again and find out what he wants to say.'

'I think I already know what he wants to say,' announced Gloria.

'To identify his murderer?' suggested Dunster-Dunstable, looking thrilled.

Gloria shook her head. 'Something more important.'

Kingfisher turned to Count Marred. 'What d'you make of all this?'

Count Marred had been lurking behind the crowd in the small room. He looked thoughtful for a moment, then shouldered his way forward and stood in front of the flushed-looking Gloria.

He seized her hand. 'I say this is tremendous news. What a breakthrough. Did he really try to speak?'

'He was just a shadowy shape. He was gone in an instant.'

'And it was definitely Dr Thallomius?' sneered Kingfisher. 'Short guy. Old fella.'

Gloria scowled at him. 'It was like a grey shadow. But it can only have been Dr Thallomius, can't it?' She stamped her polished black shoes again. 'I've told you, he has a strong connection to my family.'

'Where was this presence?' asked Angelique.

Gloria waved at the corner and everyone looked to where she pointed – the part of the room that was dominated by a life-size portrait of a woman dressed in black with a sour face and disapproving eyes.

Everyone stared at the scary woman in the picture, who looked like she'd never had a day's fun in her life. Seth wondered how anyone could possibly sleep with that face watching your every move and guessed the same thought had occurred to everyone.

'I am sure that picture would spook anyone,' said Count Marred gently, starting to move away.

But Angelique began to feel all around the frame, even peering behind it. 'Was the shape actually in the room?'

'I didn't just get spooked by a portrait,' said Gloria defensively.

Angelique was brushing her hands over the

surface of the portrait. Seth guessed she was dying to zap it with her divinoscope, but knew she wouldn't dare with so many people around.

Professor Papperspook leant towards Count Marred excitedly. 'This really is a most exciting development in Gloria's magic. I suggest we test her abilities. See if she can contact him again.'

'What do you mean?' Kingfisher interrupted.

'We need to talk to Dr Thallomius. I suggest we hold a seance.'

## 33. A SECRET

Kingfisher barked out a laugh and Gloria Trout-bean's colour turned from angry uneven crimson to an ill-looking white.

'I may be young and my magical powers may not be well developed. But I come from an ancient magical family. I could tell the lot of you things about the Sorcerer General that would shock you,' snapped Gloria, her eyes flashing. 'I know why he wants to talk to me. I expect he wants to apologize.'

Count Marred turned. 'What for?'

Gloria spoke again, her voice had grown shrill. 'It's time you all listened to me. Dr Thallomius came through to me because I know Dr Thallomius's secret.'

'His secret?' echoed Marred.

She swung around, jabbing an accusing finger randomly. 'My grandfather invented one of the cleverest magical devices of the age and he was cheated out of getting the credit for it by Dr Thallomius!'

'Don't say too much, dear,' muttered Papperspook, starting towards Gloria, who was being crowded by Count Marred and Kingfisher.

'That's enough, Professor Papperspook. I'm sick of listening to your advice. You made me put on those ridiculous shoes.' She turned and stamped her foot. 'You interfered and didn't believe I had a talent to get me past the Prospect and into the Elysee. But seeing the dead is my magical power and I'm not going to be cheated out of getting recognition for my magical gifts.'

'Do be careful what you are saying,' said Professor Papperspook, finding herself shut out by the crowd.

'What secret?' said Angelique.

'Yes, tell us,' said Darinder Dunster-Dunstable.

Gloria looked around, her hands clasped together in front of her, her eyes flashing. 'Ah, now you are listening.'

Professor Papperspook, peeping under Count Marred's arm that barred her way, said, 'I'm sure they don't want to be bothered, dear.'

Gloria ignored her, enjoying herself, 'You all know the famous story of how Dr Thallomius and my grandfather, Wintergreen Troutbean, were best friends when they were young. Everyone laughs at the crazy inventions, the pranks. But do you really know why they fell out?' Her eyes had narrowed to slits, a triumphant smile on her face. 'It is a terrible story.' Gloria was making the most of this. 'Dr Thallomius, the one everyone goes on about being so utterly marvellous. Well it is time everyone knew what he was really like.'

'No Gloria!' shouted Professor Papperspook, trying in vain to reach her.

But Count Marred deliberately barred her way. 'I think we should hear this.'

'There is a reason that matter is secret,' she hissed.

'My grandfather and Dr Thallomius created this device,' ploughed on Gloria, gleefully ignoring Professor Papperspook. 'But Dr Thallomius got cold feet when he realized what they'd created – its awful evil power. Then it disappeared. Torpor Thallomius accused my grandfather of stealing it and selling it for a fortune. My grandfather was never able to prove his innocence.' She drew herself up further and said in a deep and portentous tone, 'It broke his heart. Dr Thallomius was responsible for forever tarnishing the noble and ancient name of Troutbean.'

Professor Papperspook finally wrenched herself free and seized Gloria. 'So sorry, probably better to leave Gloria to have a lie down.' She attempted to shoo everyone back towards the door, but they moved reluctantly, all eyes transfixed by Gloria. 'She really doesn't know what she's talking about.'

'I don't need a lie down,' said Gloria, trying to squirm out of her grasp. 'And I do know what I am talking about.'

'But what is it?' asked Count Marred, pausing in the doorway. 'What is this device you are accusing Torpor of inventing, and then becoming scared of?'

'Didn't you know, Count, about your best friend being responsible for inventing something so wicked and feared, one of the grotesquely evil inventions of the sorcerers' world? Your marvellous Dr Thallomius invented the firefly cage.'

## 34. WE ALL KNOW WHAT HE STOOD FOR

'It's a monstrous lie,' came a gravelly voice into the heavy silence that followed Gloria's shocking statement. Everyone turned to Marred, his ruined face the picture of misery in a sea of motionless faces, frozen in a moment of shock.

'Torpor never invented that infernal device. He never could. He stood out against misuse of magic, against sinister magic of all kinds. He fought against all of that.'

'We all know what he stood for, Boldo,' said

Pewter, slapping a reassuring hand on Marred's back. 'We all know what a great man he became.'

'Became?' said the Count uncertainly. He turned to Angelique. 'You worked closely with him, Miss Squerr. Wasn't he the kindest, most generous? Helping magical people make the most of their magic and using magic as a force for good is the code he lived his life by. He simply would not have been capable of inventing that atrocious device.' His hands moved in deep agitation.

'Well, who can honestly say they didn't invent something of immense deadly power and brutality in their youth?' put in Pewter, mildly, as if saying something reassuring. 'You show me any great sorcerer and I will show you someone with secrets. Sometimes taking a wrong path in your youth sows the seed of greatness.'

Seth had to fight an urge to react with a sudden burst of laughter after all the tension and had to cover it with a cough.

'You think it's true that his inventions were once evil? You believe he did do this monstrous thing – he was the inventor of that abomination – the firefly cage?' went on Marred.

'I think,' said Angelique thoughtfully, 'that using magic for good means resisting the powerful pull of sinister magic, Count Marred.'

'Who can be both wise and young?' said Pewter cheerfully. 'Making your mistakes early leads to wisdom beyond your years, isn't that what they say, Boldo?' he slapped Count Marred again on the back. 'Who cares about his sinister past?'

Seth looked at Marred's face. If it had shown devastation at his friend's death before, it now looked even more haggard at hearing such a terrible accusation.

'You look like you could do with a sit down, sir,' suggested Seth to Marred. 'Why don't you head for the hotel lounge. I'll make you some tea,' he offered, receiving Pewter's glance with a nod.

He was glad of a reason to slip away, much as he longed to hear anything more that was said about whether the other guests believed this accusation of Dr Thallomius having a sinister past.

But he hadn't forgotten he was supposed to be keeping an eye on Mr Bunn. And he suddenly realized that Mr Bunn hadn't come running when Gloria screamed. So where was he?

And had Nightshade had any luck? Was she any closer to finding out if Mr Bunn was magic or a trickster? Had she got anything to tell him?

He decided that no one in the lounge would

notice if their tea took a little longer to fetch. He just needed a little time. Where would Nightshade be now? Hopefully she wouldn't have just fallen back asleep on his bed, she would be on the trail.

He moved stealthily through the lobby and paused by the welcome desk. Behind it was a tapestry picture of a girl in a pretty yellow dress that concealed the secret entrance to where Mr Bunn had a tiny study.

Was it possible that Mr Bunn was in there right now? Seth tried to picture him sitting there poring over magical text books and practising spells in secret. Could he catch him right now? He hadn't seen Mr Bunn for ages.

He crept behind the welcome desk and tried to listen for any telltale signs that the room was occupied.

He pushed aside the tapestry and moved the tiny door just enough so that he could see that the room was in complete darkness. No one was allowed in here. Seth had never got further than looking from the doorway. He had always assumed Mr Bunn spent his days here as idly as possible, skulking quietly, leafing through a newspaper, taking a nap.

But had Mr Bunn recently been in here secretly finding a way to do magic?

'Aren't you supposed to be in the kitchen?' a voice behind him snapped.

Seth jumped, turned and caught a whiff of Norrie Bunn's rum-laced breath on his cheek and raced into the kitchen before she could even begin to yell at him.

He reluctantly slumped his way to the kettle. How was he going to find any time to do any sleuthing? How was he going to find Mr Bunn? Seth could only hope Nightshade had had better luck.

And then he found Mr Bunn.

He was there, right in front of him, at the sink, tackling the enormous pile of washing up very, very slowly, almost in a daze.

Seth kept his head down as he assembled cups and the biggest teapot he could find, constantly darting looks at his employer and thinking how he could bring up a conversation about how on earth Mr Bunn had been secretly practising magic. How had he made Henri's little carved bugs come to life? Seth burnt to know the truth, but how could he get the truth out of Mr Bunn?

It had to have been a trick, one that was good enough to fool even Angelique. But it was so difficult to believe Mr Bunn had managed that. How had he done it?

As Seth slowly filled a jug with milk and gathered everything together on a tray, he went through everything in his mind once again as he tried to hit on an answer that made sense of everything.

He turned to Mr Bunn, a question on his lips about whether his employer was really a sorcerer, but he only noticed how lined and saggy his face was, as his hands rhythmically soaped a plate over and over in the foamy water. Instead of seeing the lazy man he had worked for all these years, Seth tried really hard to see a powerful sorcerer.

'Ah Seth. All these visitors,' Mr Bunn said, wiping his brow and leaving a trail of bubbles. 'They don't really believe you poisoned the old fella, do they? They wouldn't really take you away?'

'I don't know, sir. There is a lot I don't know. This place is beginning to seem almost a mystery in itself.'

He stopped as he picked up the heavy tray loaded with the giant teapot, cups and jug of milk into the hallway. And realized these were almost exactly the same words as Angelique had been saying to him right from the beginning – that all the answers were here, at the hotel, before the Prospect even arrived. And that Seth must have all the answers.

Only he didn't, he simply didn't.

So when he saw a figure moving at the top of the stairs, Seth just slid the tray quickly on to a low table in the lounge, and slipped straight back out again to follow quietly up the stairs.

## 35. WATCHING THE TRAGEDY UNFOLD

He hovered in a shadowy space and watched.

Angelique was working her way along each of the paintings on the first-floor landing, running her fingers deftly around each one in turn. Seth watched, fascinated, from the shadows as a flash of blue light lit up the landing and Seth saw her frown as she took out her red notebook to write something in it.

'Seth. What can you tell me about the paintings?' she said, without lifting her eyes from the notebook.

'Err – I . . .' Seth stepped out of the shadows, embarrassed. The woman in the mad hat grinned at him from the painting at the end of the corridor.

'I don't know anything, really I don't. But what are you doing, Angelique? Do you think the paintings have got anything to do with – anything?' he finished lamely.

'Good question, Seth. Do you think they are connected?'

'To the murder?'

'Well I thought maybe to each other.' She bit her lip and frowned. 'There is something strange here; something else that I don't understand.' She stowed the notebook in her ruby handbag and flipped closed the silver top of her cane. 'I keep telling you that you have more answers than you realize.' She moved closer, her dark eyes flashing dangerously. 'I just can't work out if you actually think it is a good idea to keep it all to yourself.'

He rubbed his neck as he recalled Angelique pressing in with the end of her bewitching cane the last time he'd let slip that he knew anything at all.

That's what had happened last time he had mentioned a firefly cage, but now he had no choice but to risk mentioning it again. He was now desperate to know. What exactly was a firefly cage? Why had everyone reacted with such deep horror when it was mentioned?

Angelique had told him Dr Thallomius used to be a scientific inventor, and Kingfisher had confirmed Dr Thallomius used to invent with Wintergreen Troutbean.

But could kindly Dr Thallomius truly be the inventor of some sort of horrible magic? What did it do?

'That firefly cage that Gloria mentioned . . . the one she says Dr Thallomius and her grandfather invented . . . what does it actually do that is so terrifying? You have to tell me now, what exactly is a firefly cage? Why is everyone so shocked?'

He heard Angelique suck in a rapid breath. But at least this time she made no attempt to shower him with those lethal-looking blue sparkles for merely mentioning it, even though he found he'd tensed himself for that to happen.

'It's a prison. It's a particularly cruel way of imprisoning a sorcerer,' she told him quietly, flipping the silver top on her cane. 'Their body is trapped, but there is one thing that is still free. Their magic. Seth, it's horrible. It means if someone traps a sorcerer in a firefly cage, then someone else can access their magic.'

It was difficult for Seth to imagine exactly why that should be so horrible, but he could see it was something that struck terror into the hearts of people with magic.

But what was really troubling him now was why had the firefly cage been written about in the black book?

As he headed for the lounge to refill the teapot, Seth could tell they had all been discussing something important by the way Pewter, Marred and Kingfisher looked up.

Angelique had followed him in and she took one of the squashy seats gathered around the low table. The room that seemed to have settled with an unshakeable gloom and Seth thought that he should probably relay the fire to cheer things up a bit.

'Miss Troutbean has offered us a seance and I must say, what a totally terrific idea,' announced Pewter. 'Shall we say the dining room in one hour? Mr Kingfisher, if you could see to the necessary arrangements? Excellent!'

Kingfisher didn't look happy about it, but he got up to go and do as he was told.

'My feeling is that if Dr Thallomius's undead spirit is wandering the hotel, we would track it down there,' ruminated Pewter, drumming his long fingers on the table. 'I think it might be very revealing.'

Marred nodded his head heavily. 'Anything you think that will help clear up this awful mystery and mess.' He mopped his brow.

The sound of familiar tiny footsteps made Seth tense.

Tiffany arrived in the room, her skin gleaming, her face beaming. All heads turned and Seth knew something bad was coming when she turned to him with that slow evil grin that made him quail.

'I've just a few things to show you. I think you'll find them fascinating,' she said, addressing the room with a girlish giggle. 'I don't know if any of this might help. I do hope so.'

And on to the table in front of everyone, before he could even begin to guess what was coming, Tiffany tossed Seth's black book.

# 36. Gilbert's Extra-Strong Pickles

Seth stared at it. It just lay there and he had to fight an urge to snatch it up before anyone else got to it. Any minute now someone would pick it up and discover the recipe for apricot delice and the picture of a firefly cage.

Tiffany looked towards Seth, her face a vile mixture of contempt and triumph. She also had something else in her hand he recognized and all he could do was watch as, almost in slow motion, his life's savings kept in the old *Gilbert's Extra-Strong*

*Pickles* jar rolled across the table, continuing its noisy journey until it fell on to the floor with a crash, depositing the coins across the carpet.

Tiffany had been in his room. It didn't surprise him that Tiffany knew all about his secret hiding place. Now his small hoard of precious possessions were spilt out and everyone had come over to see. Even Kingfisher had returned already as if keen to be there to see Seth's shame.

Tiffany leant forward and picked up the one coin that stood out, holding it in her fingers so that it caught the light and glinted.

The gold coin he had been given by Dr Thallomius. She tossed it to Kingfisher.

'What's this?' he demanded.

'Tips,' replied Seth sullenly. He felt sweat prickling uncomfortably at the back of his neck.

'A gold coin as a tip for the saucepan scrubber?' scoffed Tiffany.

'It was from Dr Thallomius,' said Seth quietly. 'For taking him tea.'

Mrs Bunn snatched the coin from Kingfisher and examined it closely. 'This is a gold coin. Have you any idea how much it's worth? A gold coin? For taking tea?' Her eyes narrowed, making her pointy face look full of spite.

Kingfisher took back the coin and rolled it in his fingers and turned to Pewter. 'Seth never stops lying does he?'

Seth looked at Tiffany and could see a slow trickle of dark scarlet blood running from a short horizontal cut on her cheek. He wondered where that had come from.

He focused on inching towards the black book. If anyone saw that picture of a firefly cage, he'd be in trouble. Who would believe him that he knew nothing about magic and that he had never even heard of Dr Thallomius?

'You do all know what this is?' said Tiffany sweetly, taking back the coin. 'I'm afraid it looks like Seth stole this from Dr Thallomius. He must have stolen the coin and knew Dr Thallomius was going to expose him as a thief. Do you know what we have here?' Her eyes were full of an exultant fire, her smile wide as she barked her hateful laugh. 'Now we know why Seth killed Dr Thallomius! To stop him accusing Seth of stealing.'

'I didn't steal it.'

He had to get to that black book before anyone read it.

But Tiffany caught on to what Seth was doing

and as he moved to pick it up, she lunged, just beating Seth to it.

'And what have we here?' she scoffed, snatching up the very tatty-looking black book only held together with its scarlet thread.

As she'd reached forward, Seth noticed that the back of her hand was scored with long parallel scratches, glistening with tiny droplets of blood that matched the cut on her face. It looked like she had been in a fight. . . and there was only one opponent Seth knew would leave long scratches like that.

He felt his insides boiling with rage. 'What have you done to my cat?' he said through gritted teeth, almost throwing himself across the room to wrestle the truth from her.

But she'd already started flicking through the book. Her eyes lit up with exultant glee and she started to read out some of the worst of the weird hand-written notes and scribbles. And it must be completely obvious to everyone listening what Seth wished he'd noticed right away – that the notebook contained notes about sinister magic.

'Ooh, what do we have here, this looks fascinating, a picture of something called a firefly cage. I thought that was very nasty magic indeed, Seppi – what have you got to say about that?'

The look on her face told Seth everything he needed to know about just how much she was enjoying this.

'A firefly cage?' Kingfisher raised his eyebrows and took a look at the book.

'What have you done to my cat?' Seth yelled again.

Tiffany's dazzling blue eyes narrowed. 'Oh don't worry. I dealt with her. That manky creature won't be giving you a reason to steal from the kitchens any more, Seppi.'

'What other artefacts of sinister magic have you been hiding? Empty your pockets,' demanded Kingfisher.

Seth's tunic had a lot of pockets. He had leather pouches where he gathered herbs when he saw them growing in the garden. He laid these on the table alongside a ball of string, a paperknife and a tiny torch. And a potato peeler. He'd forgotten he'd put that there. And an awful lot of mushrooms. But then his fingers were fumbling in one of his deepest pockets and found something so curious he didn't even know what it was.

He drew out an object and frowned at it, until he recalled where it had come from. It was that weird nut which Professor Papperspook had told him had dropped on to her from the shrubbery.

As he held it now, his fingers found something unexpected. It had a lid. A disguised bottle made out of a nut, he thought, even more fascinating.

He handed it over and watched as Kingfisher peered at it and removed the lid.

The aroma released took Seth immediately to that awful moment the night before in the dining room, watching the tragedy of Dr Thallomius's death unfold. The circle of shocked faces surrounding the figure lying on the floor. And that smell. The smell he now associated with death.

Professor Papperspook had given the disguised bottle to him. Now he understood why she had winked at him like that when she told him to dispose of it more carefully.

Professor Papperspook thought he was the one who'd thrown it out of the window and it had got caught in the shrubbery. She had been trying to help him cover it up.

Seth opened his mouth to say something to defend himself, but no words came. The determined glint in Kingfisher's eye told Seth that Kingfisher had also worked out exactly what it was. But before either of them could speak a shaft of light shot out of the book, so blinding that it forced Seth to look away.

It disappeared as suddenly as it had arrived, like

the brightest torch beam switched on and off again. But Seth could just about make out something still glowing, a gleaming imprint on the book's spine where it had been blank before.

Kingfisher dropped the book and Angelique moved quickly across to seize it and put her nose close enough to read, 'It says "Wich Wracht".'

She looked at Seth searchingly. But he had no answer, no idea what it meant and as she said the words there came an echo, low and hissed that seemed to leak out of the walls, making the whole room vibrate and rumble. *Wich Wracht.*

'What was that?' asked Tiffany, her eyes shifting about her, wide with alarm.

Now everyone looked towards Seth, who could only mutter that he had absolutely no idea.

Tiffany sped to snatch the book back from Angelique, taking her by surprise and, dodging out of Angelique's way, quickly turned the pages. Then her eyes lit up triumphantly.

'Well, well, well, this is most exciting. A recipe for – what's this? Apricot delice, Seppi? Don't tell me this is the book you got that recipe from? No wonder Dr Thallomius dropped down dead the minute he ate it. And just think, Seppi, you tried to put the blame on me.'

# 37. Someone with Serious Magic

Seth sat on the upturned bucket. He was locked in the cupboard again. He drew his hands through his unruly hair. This was it, then. What chance did he have of ever clearing his name? And what exactly had happened to Nightshade?

He felt sick. He looked so guilty. Kingfisher could really not be far now from getting his wish of taking Seth away from here in handcuffs. Surely he was never going to convince anyone it was all just a series of misunderstandings and that he really wasn't guilty of anything.

What was he going to do?

The only thing he could cling on to was the fact that he hadn't done it. Someone else had. He had to work out who it was and prove it.

Did he have answers? He really should have by now. But did it really matter anyway, he thought despairingly, because how on earth could Seth prove anything now from the wrong side of the cupboard door?

He'd listened to everyone. His mind was still on Mr Bunn and how had he found a way to do such impressive magic, because that was still a mystery. Angelique had told him right from the start he had answers. He needed answers right now and he was already out of time. *Think, Seth. Think.*

He heard muffled footsteps passing through the lobby. Nightshade? Seth put his ear to the door, hoping for the sound of a friendly voice, a sign that his cat was all right. He took comfort at least in knowing Nightshade was pretty good at taking care of herself.

He caught the drift of a conversation between Tiffany and her mother as they passed through the lobby.

'Dad is magic,' Tiffany was saying, Seth could

picture her porcelain face creased in a determined frown, 'And no one thought to tell me.'

'Your father's not magic, sweet pea.'

'Do you never think? Did no one think I might want to become magic?' Tiffany was breathing hard. 'I mean – are you really that stupid?'

'Honestly, sweetness, there is nothing to tell. It's not possible, sugar pie.'

They drifted off and Seth was left thinking that he wasn't surprised Tiffany was angry. From the first moment Seth had learnt that Mr Bunn somehow had the ability to bring Henri's wooden figures to life, he had wondered what Tiffany would do when she found out. If there was any magic around here, Tiffany would definitely think it should be hers.

At the root of everything was magic. Pewter had suggested that someone seriously skilled at magic had tricked their way into the Prospect. Someone with a plan. Someone who could get past charmed doors.

Angelique had told him there was magic already here at the hotel. Distorted magic. Magic she didn't understand, she'd called it. She'd told Seth the mystery had started long before Dr Thallomius got here. So what was the answer?

Mr Bunn had found a way to get those figures to

come to life. Was it really that Mr Bunn had done incredible magic? Or was it just a trick? Or an accident? It had certainly convinced Angelique.

None of it made sense. But he had to make sense of it.

Pewter was convinced Dr Thallomius hadn't come to the Last Chance Hotel just to look at the latest candidates for recruitment and that it was all about something else, some crazy idea that Thallomius had a secret agenda. Pewter was certain that tiny piece of magical bone on top of the wardrobe was the breakthrough clue to the whole mystery.

Seth tugged his hands through his hair again. Could that really fit in anywhere? Sometimes Pewter seemed to be eccentrically lost in his own ideas, sometimes Seth doubted he was any good as an inspector at all.

Who could have done it? Who possessed a level of magical ability that meant they were capable of getting into the dining room? That's what it really came down to.

Who here was truly magical?

Had he seen anyone doing magic? Serious magic. *Think, Seth.*

At that very moment things crystallized like a blurred picture coming into focus.

He'd seen jets of fierce blue light zapping out of the end of her cane. He'd known from the start when she'd been flashing about using that dangerous cane and pressed it right into his neck that she was doing magic.

She'd pretended to be his friend and dragged Seth into keeping her secrets.

How had Seth been so stupid? So trusting?

It had stopped him seeing what he should have spotted right from the start. He knew exactly who was by far the most magical person here. There was one obvious person and it wasn't Mr Bunn at all.

It was so ridiculously obvious. It was Angelique.

# PART THREE

# 38. A Lesson in Slicing

He couldn't go to Kingfisher or Pewter without some evidence, not if he stood any chance of convincing them, because they were simply going to think he'd say anything, make up anything, just to save himself. How on earth was he going to out-manoeuvre Angelique? Could he get her to admit it all?

He was busy brewing up all his resentment about just how she had played him along and tricked him, when a small voice outside the cupboard said,

'Are you OK, Seth?'

It was all he could do not to yell at Angelique right away.

'I'm just fine. Looks like I'll get my wish to get away from here. Take the blame for what someone else has been up to. It's what I'm good at. Hope whoever really did it can live with that.'

'You need to help me, Seth.' Seth could hear her more clearly now. She must have moved closer to the door. It wasn't the first time she'd asked for his help. But he simply wasn't going to be duped any more.

'This place is very old,' she went on. 'Seriously full of secrets. I'm getting closer, but I need to know everything. Seth?'

'Why should I help you?' he spluttered angrily. 'You've lied to me and tricked me.'

She paused. 'I had no choice.'

'I know what's really going on, finally, Angelique,' he said through clenched teeth. 'How much have you been laughing at me?'

There was a long silence.

'Seth. I know things are difficult for you. But will you help me? It's important,' she breathed quietly. 'There's no one else.'

'What can I do? I'm locked up. Anyway, I don't

want to help you. You are on your own and can't use me in your plans any more.'

'N-not help me?' she spluttered. 'But I want to help *you*.'

'I wouldn't help the person who murdered Dr Thallomius, not for anything.'

He hadn't meant to say it, but it was out there now. There was such a long silence, Seth thought he'd completely blown it and she'd gone away. He'd meant to be so wily and careful and get her to talk and cursed himself for letting his anger get the better of him.

But at the end of the long silence she said, 'It is so difficult to know where to begin,' whispering so low he could barely hear. 'But the fact he's dead,' he heard she was sniffing, 'you're right, it's down to me.'

She'd admitted it.

Seth didn't know why, but he didn't feel in the least bit triumphant. And then he heard footsteps and she was gone. He was hardly any better off than he had been before.

Who would ever believe him?

It was a long time before he heard more footsteps. He put his ear to the door.

'Ah. Look, young Fishfinger might have dropped this big old iron key. I wonder what it opens.' There was the scratching sound of the door being unlocked. Seth blinked in the light of the lobby as he crept nervously out of the cupboard, and was staring up at the looming figure of Inspector Pewter.

'Thought you might need to stretch your legs. Want to come see something? Help me? Just a dull task, I'm afraid.'

'Was the key really right there?' asked Seth.

'Not exactly.'

'You. . . you used magic?'

'I might have used an unlocking spell. Simple, but effective. Doesn't change the fact that using magic is not for performing tricks, young Seth. The path to magic is one of the most difficult, treacherous and dangerous you could choose to go down. Particularly in untrained hands, magic can be – well, we have a whole department who spend their time re-attaching the ears of people who use magic without quite knowing what they are doing. And heads. Although, heads not so often. Thankfully people are usually pretty careful with their heads.'

Seth followed Pewter up the uneven stairs, watching him duck where the ceiling got really low. 'Might I suggest you concentrate less on magic and more on getting yourself out of this spot of trouble? Pretty good at that aren't you, Mr Seppi, getting yourself into trouble.'

'Spot of trouble,' Seth laughed hollowly. 'There's so much evidence against me everyone thinks I did it, nothing's going to make any difference. Can you . . . do you know if Nightshade is all right?'

'That cat? Wasn't too keen on Miss Bunn getting hold of that black book of yours.'

'What has Tiffany done to her?'

'Managed to shut her in a box. But not without a little damage to the fair skin of Miss Bunn. Night-shade was fine, once I found her and let her out. A little grumpy.'

'Yes, she's often like that. Thank you.'

They arrived at one of the bedrooms that had stood empty.

Pewter slipped inside without switching on the light and Seth followed him. Not for the first time, Seth had a sense that Pewter was in pursuit of some odd trail of his own.

'Now, let's see if we can't finally solve this mystery between us. We are close!'

Seth knew he had to find a way to convince Pewter of the extraordinary confession Angelique had just made to him, but he didn't know where to begin.

If he imagined himself saying the words, he only

imagined Pewter laughing. She really had played a clever game. It was taking a few moments for Seth's eyes to adjust and he realized the room wasn't quite empty. There was something moving in a dark corner. A grey mist was hovering.

Seth tensed and went to grab at Pewter's arm.

Could this be the same grey shape Gloria Trout-bean had seen? Was this the ghost of Dr Thallomius?

But Pewter wasn't concerned in the slightest and strode towards the small, shimmering, shivering ball of dull grey light suspended above the desk. Pewter peered curiously into its depths and Seth's fear quickly gave way to curiosity.

'I just need to tidy up some loose ends that will help my case.'

'Your case against me?'

Seth waited and hoped. It was impossible to ever know what Pewter was thinking, but somehow, from the start, when no one else seemed to believe Seth's innocence, Pewter had seemed to see further and deeper and to be seeking something else.

Pewter turned from the glowing globe to look at Seth with his blue eyes, bright even in the gloom. 'You think I've asked for your help building your own case against you? You have to learn who you can trust, Seth,' he said gently. 'Some of us are only after the truth. Now, promise not to tell on me?'

Seth felt a small stirring of hope inside him that all was not quite lost. If, even after the mountain of evidence against him, Pewter still thought there might be another answer, Seth still had a chance.

As Seth's eyes adjusted to the gloom he became mesmerized by the swirling mist. At its centre was a tiny pinprick of grey light, surrounded by a swirling sphere that grew both in size and intensity as he watched. Before he could even ask Pewter about it, it had reached the size of a small football.

'What do you mean by tell on you, sir?'

'Kingfisher sealed off all communications, quite rightly. This method is very discreet. Or would be, only you've got a truly rotten signal out here. I guess it might be all the trees. So I've had to leave it brewing up a stronger connection. And it would make my life much simpler if Kingfisher didn't know about it, because parts of what I'm about to do may be ever-so-slightly illegal.'

Seth's heart beat faster at the mention of doing something ever-so-slightly illegal with Pewter. He watched the inspector swipe a hand across the mist and Seth was spellbound at the way it started to move in a new direction. It gathered and then started to spin.

'Not ready yet.' Pewter wiggled his fingers in among the glow.

The mist arranged itself into pink dots. Pewter opened his jacket, revealing again the array of tiny bottles attached to the lining. He removed one, unstoppered it with his long fingers, took out a pinch of cinnamon-coloured powder and wafted it above the mist.

Seth knew he should be focusing on finding a way to properly put the blame where it belonged, on Angelique. She had been feeding him information about the magical world and now he was starting to doubt it all. She had told him she was finding magic she didn't understand, about there being magic at the hotel. Zapping everything with blue light – and that trick she'd pulled where the walls rumbled. She was the one who made the walls say 'Wich Wracht'. He should just come out with it, tell Pewter everything. He just needed a way to tell him about the divinoscope and the zapping, without it sounding like the most ridiculous story . . . but the globe began to glow a greenish colour and all Seth could think was that he was watching Pewter doing magic.

'They upgraded it recently,' grumbled Pewter. 'Never been as good as the old version. Don't know why they have to mess with these things. I am trying a little Unpowder – kind of a magical kick-start, if your magic isn't pulling its weight as it should. We call this a teleglobe, which I stick to because it's properly named after the sorcerer who devised it and her name is quite unpronounceable. It just sounds like you're sneezing. But you can't get away from it being the greatest magical device for finding out things quickly.'

'You mean – will it tell us who killed Dr Thallomius?' asked Seth, eager and hopeful. This might be a brilliant way forward in getting Pewter to suspect Angelique.

'Magical it might be, but it's also pretty dumb – it'll only repeat what someone's already programmed into it. Now, on a hugely expensive channel like this . . .' Pewter's hands moved and images began to come clearer. 'Why don't you try it first, Seth? Got a question? Go on. Give it a whirl.'

All Seth wanted was to get to the bottom of why Angelique might have killed Dr Thallomius, because if he knew that, he could tell Pewter everything and it would sound all right and he had a chance of being believed.

'Well,' said Pewter after Seth paused. 'I have plenty of questions. You have been learning about the magical world, Seth, about the Unpleasant and all the sorcerers Missing Feared Exploded? I do wonder if we might be thinking along the same lines.'

Seth was surprised. He thought Pewter said he was building a case against someone. He'd thought Pewter was going to ask for background on whoever he suspected.

'The sorcerers wanted in connection with the Unpleasant – is that something your department, MagiCon, investigates?' he asked carefully.

'Not us, no. We at MagiCon deal with your basic, everyday crime, wrongdoing and all manner of shady goings on in the magical community. But tracking down wanted sorcerers from the Unpleasant, and declaring those sorcerers as officially alive or dead, is the responsibility of a crack team.'

'MFE sorcerers like Wintergreen Troutbean?' said Seth slowly. 'Sounds like he had a good reason to hate Dr Thallomius. I guess people only think he's dead, no one knows for sure? I guess that has to be investigated?'

'That's it exactly. Full name of the department is the Sinister Speculation Services, although it's usually referred to as S3. But that is what they do. Most of it is undercover. Well, the last thing they'd want to do is alert a sorcerer that they are being investigated. That sorcerer may be very skilful in hiding to avoid having to answer too many awkward questions about their role in the Unpleasant. In fact, the S3 could stand for Seriously Sassy Sorcerers. Want to know more about the Elysee's team of secret agents?'

Seth peered over Pewter's shoulder, where words were beginning to emerge out of the mist.

As the words appeared, the teleglobe began to talk in a low, female voice. '*The work of the S3 begins by targeting homes or buildings connected to MFE sorcerers. They investigate use of magic. If they find no signs of recent magical activity, they conclude that the sorcerer is dead, rather than missing, and their official status is changed.*

'*Then they sweep out all the magic from the dark corners of their homes, remove magical texts, any magical artefacts, sometimes whole libraries. And once all traces of magic have been removed, then the house is said to be "cleaned" and can be declared safe for re-use.*'

'Tricky work. Guess it must backfire occasionally,' Pewter said thoughtfully. 'If the sorcerer has just been taking a long vacation.'

Seth was taking all this in, but Pewter was already swiping again across the surface and the swirling mist inside the shimmering globe turned a deep shade of pink.

'Now this is the bit which is highly illegal. And takes a little skill. Although really very simple for an absolute genius like myself. You may turn away if you wish. Slicing.'

'Slicing?'

'It's the term used for slipping unseen to dig around where you have no business to be in the first place. In this case, the Elysee vaults. They aren't that keen to let just anyone in.'

'Why?'

'I guess they think their vaults are private.'

'No, I mean—'

'Ah. I also have some tricky questions I can't answer. There are things I am being kept in the dark about. I am having no end of difficulty working out which lies I need to be bothered about,' he muttered as the mist moved and gathered. 'And I would really like to find out exactly what she is up to.'

Seth hit upon that word 'she' and a spark of hope lit inside him that it might not sound quite so ridiculous if he told Pewter about Angelique's confession.

As the name of the person Pewter was investigating emerged through the mist, Seth breathed it aloud.

'Angelique.'

# 39. LYING FROM THE START

So Pewter was already suspicious of Angelique.

Could it be that Pewter, like Seth, had worked his way to the same conclusion – that she was the only one here with enough magic to get through those charmed doors?

Perhaps there was a chance Seth was going to be able to clear his name.

Pewter leant forward, 'She doesn't even work for Thallomius.'

'She's been lying about a lot of things,' Seth

mumbled, still feeling such a complete fool for being so utterly taken in by all her ridiculous stories about magic being here.

'Yes, she does that, doesn't she?' said Pewter.

Seth wanted to tell Pewter everything. Not just about how Angelique had confessed she was responsible for Dr Thallomius's death, but all that fizzing about with her red cane, flashing blue light. All the nonsense about ripples and unexplained magic. He'd been so stupid, but he still hadn't a clue what she had done it all for or what it all meant.

'I can only think of a couple of reasons she would want to conceal the real facts from me and I don't want to have to dangle her upside-down for the truth,' said Pewter. 'The Squerrs are quite a distinguished line of sorcerers. So what is she up to? You think she's our murderer, don't you Seth?' said Pewter quietly.

Seth replied slowly. 'I can do better than that – I know she is.'

'What's she been telling you?'

'Just now she confessed to me that the fact that Dr Thallomius is dead is down to her.' Seth held his breath. There, the news was out. How would Pewter react?

Pewter turned and Seth again caught the intense

blue of his eyes behind his glasses. 'Did she indeed? Believe that, did you? She's never been anything other than completely straight with you?'

'Absolutely not!' Seth blustered. 'She's been lying to me and misleading me right from the start.'

'Yes, she plays her own game pretty close, doesn't she?'

Was that all Pewter was going to do or say?

Seth wasn't sure if Pewter didn't believe him, or whether it was completely the opposite and it wasn't news to him at all. He just seemed his usual calm self and had not reacted the way Seth had expected to the shocking news of Angelique's confession.

But then when did Pewter ever react the way anyone expected?

But something else sank in that Pewter had just said, 'So she comes from one of the old magical families?'

'One of the oldest, the Squerrs,' nodded Pewter.

Hadn't she been explaining to him right from the start how powerful magical families had been plotting to get rid of Dr Thallomius and his reforming ideas?

Seth almost missed the sound of light footsteps approaching.

Then Pewter's head turned as someone called his

name. 'Never a moment's peace. No wonder this case is taking so long to crack. But it is finally building nicely.' He slid into the corridor, pulling the door discreetly behind him.

What did he mean? Was the case not closed?

'Madam, how may I be of assistance?' he heard Pewter say, and the unmistakeably high voice of Gloria Troutbean replying as she announced: 'I am ready for the seance. But I want to know,' she sounded a little nervous, 'what questions should I ask?'

Something brushed Seth's legs. He hadn't even noticed her slip in.

'Nightshade! Where have you been?'

He went to hug her, wanting nothing more than to bury his face in her soft fur. But Nightshade gave an enormous stretch and a big yawn, unfurling her claws. 'Think I might have dropped off. Just a little . . .' she yawned widely again, '. . . nap.'

'You've been *sleeping*? I thought you were—'

'I can't help it if I need my sleep,' said Nightshade, starting to lick a paw. 'Cats need at least seventeen hours sleep a day. I'm only doing what is natural.'

'I thought something awful had happened to you – I thought Tiffany—'

'I gave her something to think about.' Nightshade

turned her back as if she didn't want to talk about it and hissed at the globe of mist. It was wriggling around, almost as if it was beckoning to Seth, *come on, give me a try*. 'Did I miss anything?'

'That, Nightshade, is a magical device called a teleglobe. You can ask it stuff. You only missed Tiffany giving the black book to Kingfisher as evidence against me. I got locked up again. But now I don't think it's Mr Bunn who is the one really responsible for all of this. I think Pewter and I might be thinking along the same lines that—'

'Don't know, Seth. There's a lot of strange things about. I'm beginning to think that Angelique might be right. There could be something dark lurking here at the hotel.'

'Huh! Well, I am learning not to trust a word that girl says. Listen, she told me just now – I asked her outright and she admitted it – she's the one responsible for Dr Thallomius's death. But I was the only one who heard her confess, although I think Pewter is doing the same as me, trying to get some evidence against her.'

Nightshade was looking at him as he moved closer to the teleglobe, her green eyes gleaming. 'And this is going to get us the evidence?'

'Gotta be worth a try. It's a magical device,'

shrugged Seth, 'Don't suppose it would work for me.' But he lifted his eyes to watch it and moved closer, transfixed by the swirling haze, which then reached out long, thin misty tendrils, grey, swirling around him, drawing him to it, pulling him in invitingly.

Seth sensed if Nightshade had any eyebrows she would be raising them now.

He had watched Pewter carefully. There was a low conversation taking place outside the door. He stood before it nervously. Could he possibly get a magical device to work?

If Seth was going to try to use the teleglobe it had to be now. He had so many questions, so many questions it was difficult to focus on just one.

He had got too confused with which lies he had been told. He rubbed his neck, thinking of Angelique getting angry with him, her buzzing everything with the fierce blue light of her divinoscope, telling him she was detecting magic she'd never seen before. Seth thought of the walls rumbling.

One chance. Something he really wanted an answer to, something that might just help him to understand exactly what Angelique's game was. He had to ask it quickly, before Pewter came back.

He bent towards the swirling teleglobe and clearly and confidently asked his question.

'Why do the walls at the Last Chance Hotel talk?'

## 40. WHAT IS WICH WRACHT?

The mist just sat there, gently curling. Had he said it too quietly? Or just done it wrong? He frowned, glanced anxiously at the door and remembered what Inspector Pewter had done.

He took the container that Pewter had left on the table, the one containing Unpowder. Seth unstoppered it. Between the tips of his fingers he took the tiniest pinch and sprinkled it across the fog exactly as Pewter had done.

Words appeared out of the mist.

*Last Chance Hotel. Formerly Last Chance House, ancestral home of Wich Wracht — the ancient name of the famed scientific sorcerer best known for inventing the RuhnGlas.*

'Nightshade, get this! *Wich Wracht* is a person!'

'What are you talking about?' grumbled Night-shade.

'That writing that gleamed out of the black book – and when the walls said "Wich Wracht". It isn't a thing. The walls were saying a name. The name of a scientific sorcerer, like Dr Thallomius was. Wich Wracht used to live here – at the Last Chance Hotel.'

Seth peered again at the words and noticed that the word ruhnglas was highlighted, as though if you wanted to, you could ask it to tell you more. What's more, he recognized the word and knew exactly where he'd seen it before.

'The word ruhnglas was mentioned in the black book, along with the firefly cage.' He thought for a moment about the words Wich Wracht appearing as a bright light shining out of his black book. 'But what does it mean, Nightshade? I still haven't a clue.'

His shoulders sagged.

The answer to his question seemed only to have given him more questions.

Seth read on, scanning quickly all the details he could.

*Wanted for questioning about involvement in the Unpleasant, if alive. Official status Missing Feared Exploded.*

'Nightshade. Wich Wracht is one of the sorcerers Missing Feared Exploded. He was involved in the Unpleasant and is wanted for questioning. And he used to live here.'

'A wanted sorcerer used to live here? You're having me on.'

The creak of a floorboard told Seth now was not the time to try to puzzle it out. Pewter was coming back and before Seth knew it, was in the room.

'I have bad news for you.'

Seth waited, wondering if he'd been found out dabbling with a magical device.

'I'm afraid you'll have to stay under lock and key, although I don't see why you should be stuck in that broom cupboard. Your attic room will do.'

Pewter followed him as Seth reluctantly agreed and dragged his way to the top floor.

'Do you really think Miss Troutbean will be able to communicate with Dr Thallomius's dead spirit?' Seth whispered as Pewter gave a comforting farewell rap on the door after locking him in.

He heard Pewter give a heartfelt sigh. 'The longer you are around magic, Seth, the more you learn to keep an open mind. Plus, be useful wouldn't it, give Dr Thallomius a chance to tell us everything. But until we prove otherwise, my advice, sadly, is trust no one. Oh, except me of course.'

'So is Miss Troutbean's ability to communicate with ghosts magic? Or do you mean you think she's up to something?'

'Don't you get the impression, Seth,' said Pewter wearily, 'that everyone here is up to something?'

## 41. The Picture Becomes Clearer

Seth slumped on to the bed, thinking furiously. He was slowly aware of a gleam, an eerie glow coming from a corner of the room.

It was his mirror. The mirror that didn't always work. Only now it was gleaming.

It was the back that was shining brightly, not the glass. He turned it over and could make out bright letters. He could read the words perfectly clearly. *Wich Wracht*.

He dropped the mirror.

As he stared wide-eyed at the glowing inscription, a slithering voice came out of the walls of his room, this time in a whisper, as if it was talking only to him. *Wich Wracht.*

Apprehensively, Seth picked up the mirror and stared at it. It was just his broken mirror, which sometimes showed his reflection, but most of the time showed a reflection of what was in quite another room. If it was connected to Wich Wracht then he had to face facts – it was quite likely some sort of artefact bewitched with sinister magic.

As he peered deep into the mirror he could only watch, transfixed with amazement, as one corner started showing a bright light, which spread across the glass like a crack. The crack widened.

Seth stared at it closely, closer than he ever had done before and all of a sudden he was seeing a group of people. They were sitting around a big table in a panelled room lit by candlelight.

Seth gripped the mirror tightly and knew exactly what he was seeing in his strange mirror. He was seeing straight into the hotel dining room where the seance was taking place.

And as he peered further and further into the glass, deeper and deeper, looking at the faces, seeing Gloria Troutbean's mouth moving, but hearing no words, Seth began to have a sensation of falling.

Before he knew it, it was as if every molecule in his body was being exploded apart at the same time as he was being crushed down into a tiny, tiny tube.

He was being sucked into the glass.

It was like being shrunk and stretched at the same time. He reached out, trying to stop himself. Seth had his eyes closed, there was a rushing sound in his ears. When he opened them again he was no longer falling. He was quite still and he seemed to have landed upright. He blinked a few times.

He looked about him, not at all sure where he was. His own hand appeared shadowy and grey and he felt as flat as a piece of cardboard. And he was looking straight into the dining room. But from where?

He could see the guests seated around the large, polished table in the centre of the room.

This is what Miss Troutbean had gathered them together for – this must be the seance. Gloria must be trying to summon the spirit of Dr Thallomius. The room was lit only by candles, just as Seth had seen when he'd looked into the glass in his room.

Professor Papperspook was sitting next to Gloria, who was directly opposite Seth. On her left was

Count Marred and then Master Dunster-Dunstable. Norrie Bunn and Henri were seated just around from the professor and just below where Seth could see out were Pewter, Kingfisher and Mr Bunn. Not Angelique or Tiffany. They were all sitting in a circle, all holding hands. But where exactly was Seth? If Pewter and Kingfisher were below him, that meant Seth was high up.

But if he had been summoned to a seance – did that mean he was *dead*? Because, really, being sucked into a glass and having all your molecules crushed like that could be enough to kill you. But he could still move.

Gloria Troutbean, who had been looking down at the table, now opened her eyes and lifted her head. She was looking right at Seth.

He made sure he didn't move, not even blink. Could she see him? Or was he now simply a spirit with no body?

Seth waited for that whooshing sensation of falling that would mean he was on the move again. But when it didn't come he tried to look to the left and the right of him.

He could see a figure to one side of him. He seemed to be between two men sharing a bottle of wine and some slices of cheese and bread. Both men, even that bread, looked familiar.

'He's here. I feel him. The presence is coming,' said Gloria.

Then Seth worked out where he must be. He was in the painting on the dining room wall, right above where he had placed the apricot dessert on the small table. He was actually standing in the painting as if he was part of it.

Gloria's eyes were now looking directly at Seth. He didn't want to be seen, especially doing something else that had the aura of sinister magic about it.

How would he ever get back to his body? What would happen if he was trapped forever in the painting?

Seth wished he knew how to make himself move.

Gloria's eyes narrowed, then opened wide with excitement. She dropped the hands of the two people sitting on either side of her and slowly got to her feet. She was moving curiously towards the painting that contained Seth and he tried to stay deathly still as her moon face creased into a curious frown.

She stared up at him, her eyes eventually locking with his, her face a mixture of curiosity and wonder. 'I can do this, I can really do this,' she said excitedly.

She extended her arm towards Seth and pointed a finger. 'There is a grey figure that's appeared in the painting. Look everyone at what I've done. I have summoned a spirit. I've done it!'

# 42. In The Land Of The Living

'I have summoned a spirit of the dead!' cried Gloria, her eyes wide.

Now everyone was turning, those beneath Seth swivelling and craning their necks awkwardly. Seth kept as still as possible, not even daring to breathe.

Everyone was scrambling to their feet, chairs scraping as they rose, their faces a mixture of interest and fear. They all moved towards the picture and were all staring directly at him.

'A spirit!' cried Dunster-Dunstable.

'She's done it!' cried the professor, clasping her hands to her mouth.

Seth felt himself move, but this time he was moving forwards not back, and there was no swirling, shrinking feeling. He felt like he was growing and taking shape and reforming and there was nothing he could do to stop himself emerging from the painting.

He carried on until he had no choice but to step over the frame, then fell in a heap on the floor. He looked up at a sea of accusing faces.

Pewter said, 'Seth.' He put out his hand to help him up. 'Nice of you to join us. Got a little bored of being on your own? It's OK everyone. He's still in the land of the living.'

'Search him!' cried Kingfisher. No one moved. Belatedly recalling he was in charge of security, Kingfisher went to grab at the dark mirror Seth was still gripping. 'What fiendish artefact of dark magic have you this time?'

'I think we might be getting to the bottom of another mystery,' said Pewter.

He extended his hand and Seth had no choice but to hand over his mirror, which Pewter examined closely. Then he leapt up and began to go over the painting, reminding Seth of how he'd watched

Angelique using her long fingers to explore the frames and the backs of all the pictures.

'How did this boy step out of a picture?' demanded Professor Papperspook, her pile of gaudy hair wobbling.

They all turned to Pewter, who was frowning at the painting.

'I think,' said Seth, dragging a hand through his hair. 'I think it is possible it might be something called a ruhnglas. I . . .' But he couldn't think of anything else he could add. How could you come crawling out of a picture holding an artefact of sinister magic and say anything that wasn't going to make it look as if you were up to no good?

'Well now!' cried Pewter excitedly, examining Seth's mirror again even more closely. 'I believe this gives us some answers! For instance, why you detected a presence in your room, Miss Troutbean.'

'You mean I didn't see the spirit of Dr Thallomius?' asked Gloria forlornly.

'It looks to me much more like it was someone wandering about using the pictures as a secret passageway,' explained Pewter. 'An outdated magical invention. Definitely banned magic. Far too many cases of people getting trapped.'

Seth was thinking furiously.

When he'd read in the teleglobe about the wanted sorcerer, Wich Wracht, having lived here at the Last Chance Hotel, and about his black book gleaming with the words, Wich Wracht, on the spine, he had started to put two and two together. Finally, he was close to seeing what was really going on.

He was only a couple of steps away from understanding everything.

# 43. LOCK ME UP AGAIN

Norrie shoved her way forward, nearly sending Gloria Troutbean flying and sticking her pointy face right into Seth's. 'What have you done with Tiffany? She's not in her room. We must find her. My poor baby.'

She looked accusingly at Seth, who could only stammer denials.

'We mustn't waste any time,' growled Henri. 'We must find her.'

'We must,' wailed Norrie. 'Something terrible

must have happened.'

'What if she's headed into the forest? We've absolutely no hope,' said Dunster-Dunstable, shrinking back. 'It's almost dark. We'd be better waiting for morning.'

'We can't wait. Perhaps she's hurt!' wailed Norrie. 'Lying injured somewhere and unable to get back. Just lying there, scared, hoping for rescue as it grows dark around her. What if she's been murdered?'

'We must leave no stone unturned,' said Mr Bunn.

'I will assist,' volunteered Professor Papperspook. 'And so will Gloria.'

'Count me in,' said Count Marred. 'Do not worry, madam. I doubt she'll be far. But may I suggest we search outside first. It will soon be getting dark.'

'Let's go!' yelled Mr Bunn.

'Thank you Count, Professor, Master Dunster-Dunstable and Miss Troutbean.' Norrie wrung her hands. 'Mr Kingfisher, can we also rely on you?'

Before he even had a chance to protest, Kingfisher got caught up in the crush, dragged out by Norrie gripping his arm and steering him to the door. Master Dunster-Dunstable on his very short legs followed last behind everyone else. Pewter announced that he would stay and keep an eye on Seth, but Seth doubted anyone would have heard.

Pewter turned to Seth, who expected to be questioned immediately about the ruhnglas. 'Well they seem very purposeful. What do you say to some tea?'

Seth could think of nothing better than a cup of tea right now and nodded gratefully, although he doubted he would ever get used to the way Pewter always asked such unexpected questions.

Pewter turned to leave and Seth followed through the deserted lobby, but as Pewter carried on into the kitchen, Seth was distracted by a strange light moving behind the tapestry picture of the girl in the yellow dress. Someone else hadn't joined in the search for Tiffany. Someone was in Mr Bunn's study. Was that strange light coming from the only other person who hadn't been at the table – Angelique? Or was it Tiffany herself?

Stealthily, leaving Pewter to make the tea, Seth headed for the welcome desk.

He had to bend to squeeze through the gap. He had never set foot in Mr Bunn's study before and he looked curiously around as he stepped right inside the small room full of shelves, some of books, but he saw mostly rows of animal skulls bleached white, with empty eye sockets. Tiny white skulls of the mice and voles that were plentiful in the woods. And a giant one with huge rolled horns.

There was a comfortable chair with worn arms and a leather seat. On a small polished table there was a pile of ancient books.

Was this where Mr Bunn had practised getting those figures to move?

The whole room was filled with the smell of scorching, as though someone had started a small fire and a figure was standing there sending snapping jets of blue light into the shelves: Angelique Squerr.

She spun around, but recovered quickly. 'Seth.'

He had no plan of what to say to her, except to let her know that her game was up and to get the final pieces to fit together. One thing he was sure of, she had been lying to him from the start. She didn't even work for Thallomius. And now he wanted the truth – the real truth this time. He opened his mouth, but the words he was about to say came out of hers.

'Time for you to tell me everything,' said Angelique.

'Me?' he said, aghast. 'It's you who has to stop pretending. I know you've been lying.'

'What on earth have you been hiding in here, Seth?' she said, as if he hadn't even spoken.

She lifted her red cane and Seth began to edge back nervously, his eyes fixed on the end as she moved towards him, her face set with that familiar fierce determination.

'Get talking, Seth. Something of immense magical power has been kept here.' The cane had started ticking.

Seth carried on edging away, not taking his eyes off Angelique as she stopped and flipped the top of her red cane. She raised the cane upwards and the ticking went frantic.

Her dark eyes narrowed. 'Tell me about it.' She sent a shower of cornflower-blue sparks into the walls.

This time the rumbling was fierce and he could hear clearly as the words Wich Wracht grumbled threateningly out of the walls.

Seth waited for plaster to start falling.

She lifted her cane up towards the ceiling and inched towards Seth, who could only close his eyes as the end glowed brighter.

He stumbled backwards, feeling behind him for something he might snatch up and use as a weapon if he needed to. But his scrabbling fingers found only small animal skulls and books.

He braced himself, waiting for the jet of blue to spark right into him.

## 44. The Truth, Pure and Simple

Seth waited until the last moment, until he sensed Angelique was really close to him. Then opened his eyes and went to grab the cane from her.

There was a movement behind him. Angelique spun to look, snatching her cane out of Seth's reach.

'Inspector Pewter,' she greeted thinly, about a second before Pewter's silvery head appeared. 'Wondered where you had got to.'

'Just a step behind you. Where I have been from the start, I fear.'

The tapestry moved aside and Seth wondered if tree-like Pewter could squeeze in through the opening.

Seth spoke quickly. 'That ruhnglas, the simple truth is I had no idea what it did. I've never used it before. It's Angelique who's got explaining to do. Do you believe me?'

Pewter emerged to stand up in the room, although his head skimmed the ceiling. 'In my experience the truth is rarely pure and never simple, Seth. And that is exactly one of the reasons I would very much like a little chat with Miss Squerr.'

Angelique held her cane up threateningly, which Pewter ignored.

'It might even be, what some people might call – long overdue. The truth, I mean.'

Angelique was standing beside the table in the centre of the room and she casually flipped open one of the books. *Demons and Witches in History.*

Seth could see the other titles. *A Concise Tome of Essential Magic-craft, Demonology, Numerology and the Zodiac. Everyman book of Magical Skills for All. Amaze your Friends! Easy Spells for Every Occasion.*

And he had thought Mr Bunn skulked in here reading the newspaper.

'You expect the truth?' she said.

'Well why not. I find it can be quite enormously helpful.'

'Seth thinks I killed Dr Thallomius. You both think I killed him?' Her eyes flashed a bold look at them both.

'You did actually tell me yourself you were responsible for his death,' pointed out Seth.

She frowned, her eyes darkened, then she spluttered. 'I told you I felt his death was down to me. Not that I actually killed him. I can't believe you both think—'

'*Did* you kill him?' asked Seth bluntly.

Angelique gasped. 'Of course not. I came here looking for – something else – but I'm sorry. There are things I am not able to tell you.'

'We know you're not really Dr Thallomius's assistant,' said Seth. 'I suppose you tricked your way here, Angelique.'

'I suppose I did, sort of.'

'Or was it his idea for you both to come here?' put in Pewter, picking up *Easy Spells for Every Occasion* from the table.

'Dr Thallomius knew I'd be interested in this place. When there was a request from someone here applying for the Prospect, it was a brilliant opportunity not to be missed. It was he who really leapt at the suggestion we travel and hold it here. But he never confided in me why he wanted to come.' She moved the cane right up to the ceiling and this time the ticking accelerated until it sounded like it was going to explode. 'Wish I'd asked a lot more questions when I had the chance. Because there was something much more dangerous waiting for him here than he expected.'

'Then he knew Wich Wracht was an MFE under investigation,' said Pewter softly. 'And the Last Chance Hotel was the last known possible sighting.'

Seth couldn't help but stare. How long had Pewter known that a missing scientific sorcerer had once lived here – and, Seth suspected, filled the place with magic, quite a lot of it sinister magic.

'I've been blaming myself for the fact that he got dragged out here where he was vulnerable. I had no idea he was in such danger,' said Angelique sorrowfully. 'The least I can do is try to find out what he came here for and try to finish whatever he was determined to do.'

'As to that,' said Pewter, 'I suspect he had a good reason of his own to see if Wich Wracht was alive or dead. I suspect what really interested him was seeing what sinister magical devices might have been left behind.'

'You came here on the trail of Wich Wracht?' said Seth to Angelique. 'You didn't come here to kill Dr Thallomius?'

'Yes, thanks for pointing that out, Seth.'

Cogs finally clicked into place. 'You are here to secretly check if the sorcerer Wich Wracht is alive or dead,' said Seth, 'I know what that means. I know what you are, Angelique, and why you can't talk about it. That makes you one of these undercover magical secret agents.'

# 45. WE SHOULD HURRY

Angelique barely flinched. 'OK Seth. Seems like my cover is blown. But just call me a cleaner, I don't really like *magical secret agent*. But now, please will you answer some of my questions?'

But Seth hadn't finished yet. 'You came here to investigate and clear the place of any sinister magic lurking here? That's what you call cleaning?'

Angelique nodded. 'And remove any magical texts or artefacts we wouldn't want to fall into the wrong hands.'

'My black book,' muttered Seth.

'Exactly. I would really like to know all about that black book,' said Angelique. 'You mentioned something to me, Seth, and I wonder if that was really where you got that information from?'

Seth hesitated, but recognized that there was little point keeping secrets any more. 'There was a picture in the black book of a firefly cage. I noticed it because it looked like the tiny birdcage I know Mr Bunn kept in here.' He pointed to an empty hook on the ceiling.

Angelique stared just for a moment, then leapt on to the polished round table. She sent another explosion of blue sparks into the ceiling, taking a reading with the end of her cane. Seth heard Pewter snap shut the book he had been holding.

'Gloria accused Dr Thallomius of inventing the firefly cage and never knowing what happened to it,' said Seth, bewildered; staring up at the empty hook. 'You mean – you can't mean that Mr Bunn's tiny birdcage was this firefly cage Dr Thallomius invented? A fearful device of awful sinister magic – here?'

'Then that was Dr Thallomius's secret mission in coming here,' cried Pewter. 'He must have guessed there was a chance his firefly cage had fallen into the hands of a scientific sorcerer like Wich Wracht. He must have been trying to track it down for years. That key he hid unlocks it.'

Angelique leapt off the table. 'You found the key to the firefly cage?'

Seth and Pewter nodded.

'Well, we found a key,' said Seth. 'I didn't have a clue what it was, but Inspector Pewter was convinced it was important and that Dr Thallomius must have brought it here for a reason. I guess he was trying to recover that firefly cage and lock it and stop anyone from using it.'

'Your Mr Bunn must have been getting his magic from somewhere.' She frowned deeply into the end of her cane. 'What's confused me from the start is that all the traces of magic should have been stale. I simply could not work out why all the readings are of distorted magic.'

Seth remembered how Angelique had explained to him how a firefly cage meant someone else could use a sorcerer's magic. Finally, he understood. That was how Mr Bunn had done magic. That was how he had made Henri's carved figures come to life. He'd been using the magic in the firefly cage.

Angelique tucked her red cane under her arm. 'There is no way Mr Bunn could have known what kind of magic he was dealing with.' She looked around her. 'If Dr Thallomius's firefly cage ended up in Wich Wracht's hands that would explain why there is so much magic around here, how magic has leaked even into the walls. But that leaves us with one big question.' She pointed to the empty hook on the ceiling. 'Where is the firefly cage now?' She went and lifted the tapestry. 'And where is everyone?'

'Tiffany's missing. They all went looking,' said Seth.

'Everyone is heading out for something called the glow-worm glade,' said Pewter, clambering through the tapestry after her. 'Sounds rather delightful. I suggest we join them.'

'Let's hurry.' Angelique headed for the lounge door at a run. 'It's an intensely powerful tool of sinister magic and one of them must have got hold of it. None of them have the faintest clue what they are dealing with.'

Angelique lifted her cane to block Seth's way.

'Not you.' She lifted her dark eyes and looked deeply into his. 'Stay here. It's way too dangerous.' She swung herself out into the darkness.

Seth would have protested, but his mind was already on another plan. Something he really needed to do.

Angelique turned back briefly. 'Did you really think I'd killed him?' Her voice was heavy with sadness.

Then she started to sprint towards the forest without waiting for a reply and he heard her voice call in the darkness. 'Let's just hope nobody else dies.'

## 46. WHO

Seth knew exactly where he was going and what he must do. He felt as if his brain must be making that same ticking noise as came from Angelique's red cane.

Just for now he would leave Angelique and Pewter to worry about the firefly cage. He was focused on another magical device completely. Something else that had been set up here by Wich Wracht.

He was convinced someone had arrived at the

Last Chance Hotel already knowing all about exactly the sort of sinister magic lurking here. Someone had arrived with a plan – a plan of how to get to the firefly cage before Dr Thallomius, get Dr Thallomius out of the picture permanently . . . and how to get away with it all very easily.

As Seth raced up the stairs he realized what a lucky escape he'd had, how close he had come to taking the blame. It had seemed impossible that anyone else but him could possibly have done it. But now he understood everything.

And if he was right, he finally also knew who had done it.

And this was his big chance to prove it.

Seth flung open the door to Room Six. He crossed straight to the desk, searching for the object that would confirm all his suspicions. To prove the truth and finally clear his own name. He knew what he had seen and it had been right here.

Now all he had to do was find it and finally prove his innocence beyond any doubt and he would be free.

'What are you thinking, Seth?'

Seth swung around and saw Nightshade had padded in silently after him.

'The pictures in the hotel are set up like a secret passage. You get into it via a magical device called a ruhnglas. It explains the mystery of how Gloria Troutbean saw a grey shape moving in her bedroom she thought was the spectre of Dr Thallomius.'

Nightshade's whiskers quivered.

'But more than that, it's the answer I've been searching for from the beginning. The answer to that question I've asked myself dozens of times without having a clue of how to answer it – of how someone got into the dining room to put the poison into Dr Thallomius's dessert. The ruhnglas must be how the murderer did it. But it's not here.' He hit the desk in frustration.

'It was Kingfisher?' said Nightshade.

'Had to be. But I have to prove it.' Seth frantically went through the objects on the desk. But the mirror definitely wasn't there. 'When I first saw it I thought it was my mirror. I picked it up. But it must have been a ruhnglas. But it's not here? How am I going to prove what he did?' he said in a panic.

Nightshade leapt up on to the desk.

'He came prepared, didn't he? Was well informed about this place,' she hissed. 'He must have known before he arrived how he'd get the run of the hotel, passing any locked or charmed doors.'

'I had the answer all this time. I should have worked out it was a magical device because it would sometimes show a view of a different room.'

'You couldn't have known, Seth. And you did work it out.'

'But how do I prove it? Without the mirror, I haven't a chance.'

'Don't worry, Seth, I think I might have the proof you need.'

She moved across the room in one slinky movement and pointed at something pinned to the back of the door. A card, like a playing card, attached with a golden pin shaped like a dagger. On the card was a picture of a red flower.

Seth slowly unpinned it and stared at the card. 'I know exactly what sort of flower this is. Red Valerian.'

'Kingfisher is Red Valerian!'

Seth considered bumbling Kingfisher and could not quite picture him as being a master criminal.

'My guess is Kingfisher was acting under orders,' said Seth pocketing the card. 'I can see this was all Red Valerian's plan to get rid of Dr Thallomius – and get hold of a powerful magical device at the same time. And so far, Nightshade, he's getting away with it.'

Something strange drew Seth to the window.

'Kingfisher took charge of sealing all the exits,' said Nightshade. 'Think he might have been smart enough to leave himself a way clear for him to escape? He might have gone already.'

Seth's stomach plummeted. 'But it can't be too late. What on earth is that?'

Out of the window and towards the glow-worm glade Seth watched a vast, vivid, almost luminous green glow.

'What the heck is it?' said Nightshade.

'I don't know, we should find out,' said Seth, a sick feeling growing. 'But it can't be good.'

## 47. AN UNEXPECTED ARMY

They plunged out in the direction of the forest where the green glow was coming from. Tonight it felt as if the dark forest had crept even closer.

The trees grew so dense that after a while they blotted out even the eerie light they were following. Seth stopped, knowing if you were out in the forest it paid to take a moment to stop, to calm your own breath and the beating of your heart, then you could start to hear things. He paused long enough to let his breath slow, to listen to the whisper of the forest.

What was it trying to tell him?

Dunster-Dunstable on his squat little legs, Professor Troutbean with her floaty dress and flappy manner, Gloria and the rest. They were all supposed to be out here searching for Tiffany. He could not imagine them wanting to hang around in a dank forest as the darkness grew, especially as the ground got squelchy and boggy as they went further from the hotel and neared the river.

So where was everyone?

He could hear no searching, no calls.

Everything was dark and eerily quiet. Faintly, in the distance, came another sound Seth recognized. The sound of rushing water carried in the night. He and Nightshade must have run far enough to reach the river. Had Tiffany been found? Had he somehow missed them and they were all in fact back at the Last Chance Hotel, sitting in the squashy chairs in the lounge, drinking tea? But where was the firefly cage?

Then the silence was broken with the piercing note of a terrified scream.

Seth battled onwards, Nightshade by his side, his feet constantly snagging roots in the dark. He almost stumbled over Pewter and Angelique, who were crouched in the thick foliage.

'What's happening?' Seth demanded.

But when he looked ahead, they didn't need to tell him. He was looking at a scene that belonged in the middle of a nightmare. Here were the Professor, Miss Troutbean, Master Dunster-Dunstable and Count Marred, along with Horatio and Norrie Bunn and even Henri. They were cowering in a circle, clutching each other, looks of terror on anguished faces that were tinged green from a strange light, but it wasn't from the glow-worms.

They were surrounded by a collection of what Seth could only imagine had once been Henri's carved creatures, whittled figures of wood and vegetables. It was exactly like Angelique had described Mr Bunn's magic, where he had made them come to life.

Only they had grown to become monsters. Gigantic creatures, blind and heavy, with lumbering clicking legs and sightless wooden eyes, their limbs flailing randomly in the darkness, forming a circle in which the small figures of guests and staff cowered in their shadows. One move from any trying to escape the circle would surely end in them being crushed.

Pewter struck up a light in his palm, bright as a match. He nursed the ball of light, cupping his hands as it turned from light to a flame, as if he was assessing what to do with it.

Seth whispered a warning, 'If you start a fire those things might burn, but chances are everything else will go up like tinder. Those people might be trapped in a wall of flame – and what if it reaches the forest?'

Pewter instantly shut off the fire.

Seth looked at Pewter and Angelique's faces, which were both tinged with the same reflective green. 'You're both magic – can't you do something to bring those creatures down to normal size?'

'There's already way too much magic around,' explained Angelique. 'Adding any more is likely to produce something horribly explosive.'

Seth turned and looked beyond the circle of petrified folk, beyond the wider circle of terrifying wooden monsters, into the darkness towards the roar of the river. There had to be a way to free them. He could just make out where the green light was coming from. Where was Kingfisher?

He moved, crouching low, and started to run, skirting the dark trees in the direction of the waterfall, taking advantage of the darkness just beyond where the light spilt, taking advantage of how well he knew this bit of the forest.

But as he got closer, Seth had to put up his arm to shield his eyes, the light was getting brighter, so bright it hurt. But he could just make out a figure. A tiny figure holding up an object that jetted piercing beams of white light. The air was filled with an over-powering smell of burnt oranges mixed with a smell like smoke after a dying fire.

Seth could see that his best chance, maybe his only chance, was to approach from behind, take the figure by surprise. And then they turned and he could see clearly who it was. They were holding a small cage, which had a beautiful golden light spilling from between its bars. The figure holding it aloft was Tiffany.

Her triumphant white face was gleaming in the mesmerizing light that was cascading from the object she was holding.

Seth inched closer. It was clear Tiffany was using the cage to control those monstrous wooden figures. Seth could see that even her parents and Henri were looking on in dread as Tiffany kept up the circle of lumbering tree-like objects, stumbling blindly like zombies, controlled by the beam of light that was being generated by the cage she held above her head.

He moved close enough to spring, knowing he could take her down.

Then out of nowhere, a fist smashed into the side of his face and sent him reeling. He saw stars, but managed not to fall.

'Seth. Been wanting to do that since we first met.'

# 48. AND I'M GOING TO GET AWAY WITH IT

'If it isn't my favourite chief suspect. I should have just left you under lock and key. Too soft, that's my trouble.'

Seth gritted his teeth and tried not to show how much Kingfisher's punch had hurt him. He knew without a doubt now that Kingfisher had killed Dr Thallomius, but now wasn't the time to deal with his anger about that, he needed to find a way to save everyone from Tiffany.

'We need to stop—' but he got no further.

He felt something grabbing at his legs, holding him. The way Kingfisher stood just a couple of feet away made Seth sure he was being held fast by magic. Kingfisher moved relentlessly closer and seized him in a swift move. He turned Seth around, twisting his arm upwards so that Seth cried out.

'Thought it would be so easy to get you to take the blame. I should have been out of here yesterday, with you in handcuffs. A job well done. Congratulations all round. You really have been a pain, Seth. Time I caused you some.'

Seth tried to twist away, but Kingfisher held him too firmly. If he didn't stop hauling Seth's arm like that he was going to black out any second.

'You killed Dr Thallomius,' said Seth, gritting his teeth.

'And I'm going to get away with it. You can't stop me. I've always been a step ahead.'

'A step ahead? Then why involve Tiffany? You had to because you were too useless to put the blame on me all by yourself. You failed.' Seth tried to wind around, but Kingfisher only twisted his arm further upwards at an angle that made Seth fear it would break. He felt the pain and sweat broke out, his vision blurring for a second, but focused on one thing. Kingfisher had killed Dr Thallomius. He absolutely could not get away with it. Seth had to find a way.

'That's your trouble, Seppi,' Kingfisher hissed in his ear. 'Always getting in the way. It's because of you I've had to scheme and backtrack and I had to involve her.' He lifted his arm to jab an accusing finger and look at Tiffany.

He was distracted enough just for a second, just a moment, but it was long enough for Seth to seize his chance to bring his booted foot down on Kingfisher's ankle, causing him to howl.

Seth had never deliberately caused anyone any pain before ever in his life. But he thought of Dr Thallomius and made a fist with his free hand. He knew he had to make this punch a good one. He had one chance. He sent it slamming into Kingfisher's face.

'That's for locking me up in that cupboard,' he said.

He managed to bring up his elbow after the punch and caught the soft part of Kingfisher's chin.

'And that's for Dr Thallomius.'

He left Kingfisher sprawled on the floor and was free to go after his next target. He sprinted. He knew he'd have only seconds, but he might still have the element of surprise on his side.

He raced towards Tiffany and would have made it if Kingfisher hadn't recovered enough to yell a warning just as Seth's spring brought him out of the shadows.

Tiffany turned and caught him at the last second, her face turning from smiling evil triumph to surprise and then shock.

Then the smile returned, an evil leer, as she saw it was Seth.

Seth just ploughed right on.

He didn't go for the cage, but, using both hands, crashed straight into Tiffany's middle, sending her staggering backwards, the look of surprise perfect on her flawless face.

She clung on and Seth moved closer, hooking one of his feet around her right leg so that she stumbled backwards and crashed heavily, face first, to the floor.

She dropped the firefly cage.

The instant she let go, Seth spun to look and saw all the wooden figures rolling on the ground, all the shafts of white light simply stopped, as if someone had pulled a switch. The giant wooden figures stopped moving, and were shrinking back to normal size, making their last sways of distorted movement, like snowmen melting.

Tiffany was on the floor and crawling towards

Seth, but he saw her and kicked out and ran to grab the firefly cage.

But now all chance to see was fading without the magical light. He could see nothing except vague shadows cast by the moon and stars and the green glimmer of the nearby glow-worm glade.

Something launched itself at Seth from side on, lunging with full force, and it was his turn to crash to the ground, crunching his shoulder into the soft mulch beneath his feet. He reached his hand forwards, stretching in the almost blackness, knowing Kingfisher was there, but neither could see in the dark and they scrabbled blindly in the dirt. Because the firefly cage was there too.

Then his fingers found it and he snatched it up and Kingfisher let out a roar of rage as he realized Seth had beaten him to it. He gave a second leap towards Seth, putting his hands around his throat. Seth tried to fight him off, looking into his crazed eyes, starting to choke, the pressure on his neck making the world blur. It was several long seconds before Seth remembered he had something to hit him with and whacked him over the head with the cage.

Kingfisher released his grip and went sprawling and Seth took in gulps of cold air, hoping everyone else was getting away and heading for safety.

Seth, bent double, his arm still aching from Kingfisher's twisting, his throat feeling like he'd swallowed sandpaper, breathed, and in the darkness saw the flash of a shadow that had to be Tiffany running away.

She was going towards the waterfall. But the river was no means of escape. The rapids here were raging. The air was already filled with their warning roar, but Seth had no choice but to scramble after her. A weak moon had emerged from the clouds, but it hardly mattered as he was nearly blinded by the spray. She was heading up alongside the waterfall itself.

Tiffany began to climb and Seth followed, one hand clutching the firefly cage. The rocks became more slippery as they got higher.

He was grabbed from behind and as he tried to find the last remnants of strength to struggle, he felt the sharp point of a blade at his throat.

'This is as far as you go, Seppi,' said Kingfisher, right in his ear, 'hand it over.' He had to yell above the roar of the angry water.

As Kingfisher used the blade to prod him closer to the edge, all Seth could do was inch backwards, still clinging on to the firefly cage, to the very edge of a rock that jutted right out over the raging flow. His eyes swivelled to see the fierce swirl of the water rushing from the waterfall.

Kingfisher and Tiffany had surprised him by heading for the waterfall. Seth wondered what their plan could possibly be. Help would be too far away even if anyone could see in the dark that they'd headed this way.

The knife glinted silver in Kingfisher's hand.

Seth had no option. He was going to have to hand over the firefly cage. Unless he let himself fall into that unforgiving water. He could do it. And he could take the dark device with him and it would be the end of both him and firefly cage. It was his only way out.

Over Kingfisher's shoulder Seth could see that Tiffany's progress was getting slower as she stumbled over the rocky ground.

But Seth caught a glimpse of something that surprised him. Closing in on her was someone who had come to find them in the darkness rather than heading for the hotel. The bulky, scarred figure of Count Marred.

Then a spark of blue zapped Kingfisher's chest and he dropped the knife as if it had become lightning. Seth turned and saw Angelique, her face set determinedly.

Kingfisher was quick and grabbed, not at Seth, but at the cage. Now they both had hold of it, neither willing to let go, grappling and slipping on the treacherous rock. Seth felt himself lose his footing and teeter back so that the rush of water was like thunder in his ears. Still he clung on.

Angelique stepped in and her cane swept low to the ground, swiping at Kingfisher's legs, Kingfisher's grip on the cage loosened, but was the only thing stopping Seth falling into the water and he felt himself tip backwards.

A hand grabbed him. A firm grip pulled him slowly away from the edge to safety and Seth found himself looking into the dark eyes of Angelique Squerr. They both turned in time to see Kingfisher already leaping away, clutching the firefly cage like a trophy.

The water was too loud for it to be heard, but Seth mouthed *thanks*.

He didn't know why Kingfisher headed for the waterfall, but Seth could see Tiffany now scrambling just a few feet ahead of Marred, heading in exactly the same direction.

Seth struggled on, fighting exhaustion. Climbing was slow and painful as he closed the gap on Kingfisher, with Tiffany just ahead and Marred and now

Angelique closing in. They were all scrabbling upwards slowly, the water soaking all of them and making it almost impossible to see.

When Kingfisher was only an arm's length ahead of him, Seth wearily launched himself. Kingfisher kicked out and started to scramble backwards across rocks, still heading higher towards the very top of the waterfall, where the water cascaded out of the hillside. But Kingfisher held on to the firefly cage.

Seth felt the full force of Tiffany careering into him from the side, knocking the breath out of him. She tried to give Seth a kick, but he reached out and grabbed her leg, jerking her off her feet. She satisfyingly face-planted into soft earth, but only turned to flash those perfect white teeth at Seth in a grin that told him he'd failed to hurt her.

He found it much easier than he thought it would be to punch her, because he had imagined himself doing it so very often. Tiffany screamed as Seth's punch connected with her nose, enough to send out a trickle of red blood.

'Look what you did to my dose, Seppi,' said Tiffany, her eyes filling with tears.

Seth left her nursing her bloodied nose and went for Kingfisher, scrabbling up the slippery rocks, his fist stinging.

Soaking wet, stained with Tiffany's blood and barely able to speak from where Kingfisher had choked him, Seth breathed heavily, still believing he could stop him and get back the firefly cage.

Then Kingfisher waved something aloft and Seth could see what it was – the black book.

Kingfisher lifted it and dangled it above the torrent of water, threatening to drop it. Seth could do it, he could reach Kingfisher. Kingfisher laughed and Seth saw his precious book curl in an arc, thrown from Kingfisher's grasp and heading straight for the pitiless river. Without thinking, Seth took his eye off Kingfisher, dived forward and caught his book, only just, in the tips of his fingers, saving it from being lost for ever in the river. And when he looked around, Tiffany, still clutching her nose, was reaching towards Kingfisher.

Kingfisher went to take her hand, but she wasn't reaching for him. She totally surprised him by grabbing instead at the firefly cage and shoved him aside, knocking him off balance. He was too shocked to stop her and, just to make sure, Tiffany sent the firefly cage slamming into the side of Kingfisher's head.

They were high now, almost at the top of the crashing waterfall, but there was something about the large, flat stone on the very edge of the roaring waterfall where Tiffany had stopped, something about the way it shimmered as if the rock itself was moving into the distance that told Seth something was wrong and that it was already too late.

Tiffany reached forward, the fingers of one hand stretching out, the other closed tightly around the firefly cage and she touched the large flat stone.

And then she wasn't there.

She had completely vanished.

## 49. THE LAST HOPE

Seth looked at the blank rock where Tiffany had literally disappeared before his eyes.

'Well,' said a voice, and Inspector Pewter appeared at his elbow, nodding at the empty rock, water dripping off his hair and off the end of his nose. 'That'll mean an awful lot of paperwork on Monday.'

Kingfisher, also drenched, hair plastered to his face, his moustache sagging, let out a cry of rage. 'She escaped in the teleport I set up! And she took the firefly cage with her! We must get after her, we've got to stop her, we—'

'You, young man, are going nowhere,' growled Pewter. 'I am arresting you in the name of MagiCon.' Pewter took from a pocket what looked like a piece of thin, green twine and Seth hoped he had something more substantial than something you used to tie up tomatoes if he was going to secure Kingfisher.

'No!' The rest of Kingfisher's rage was lost in the torrent of the waterfall. He took one look at the twine and backed away, sending out a vicious kick at Pewter, who dodged nimbly. Seth didn't even see how he got Kingfisher's hands behind his back. But as soon as his hands were tied, Kingfisher stopped yelling and struggling, and went completely silent. In fact, he stopped moving. He seemed to float like a balloon.

'Magical arrest,' Pewter explained to Seth.

They were the last words Seth remembered as his head started swimming. He felt all the pain where he had been punched and hit about the head and the tiredness from chasing through the forest and the climb to the top of the waterfall. He felt the weakness take over his legs, which buckled beneath him and he fell in a crumpled heap of exhaustion at Pewter's feet.

*

Someone had tucked Seth into bed. His first thought was to lie there for as long as possible. To snuggle back into the pillow. For ever, if at all possible. Nightshade was curled up on the end of the bed and he moved his legs slowly so as not to disturb her.

He lifted a hand with difficulty and tentatively put it to his head, which felt as if it had swelled to the size of a watermelon. It throbbed with pain as if someone was attacking the watermelon with a hammer.

He needed to know what was going on even more than he needed to sleep, so he struggled downstairs, following the sound of voices into the kitchen. His hand felt for his black book where he liked to keep it tucked inside his shirt. But someone had taken it from him. Seth moved his aching limbs painfully towards the kitchen and heard Count Marred sobbing.

'Why? Why did he have to kill him?'

'I doubt Kingfisher was smart enough for it to have been his plan.' There was the sound of Pewter quietly stirring tea. 'Following orders is my guess.'

'Red Valerian? Orders to get hold of the firefly cage and eliminate Dr Thallomius in the process?'

Seth finally reached the kitchen, which contained

only Pewter, Count Marred and Angelique.

Pewter was nodding. 'It started to go wrong when he couldn't quite pin the blame on Seth. He was operating out of his depth. Then Tiffany got the sniff of something she'd like to be involved in and even she managed to outsmart Kingfisher.'

'Tiffany always had plenty of brains, she just never found anything worth using them for before,' said Seth, speaking out and noticing the kitchen was tidy and smelt of boiled eggs and toast.

As they all wished him a good morning, Seth glanced at the cracked kitchen clock, amazed that he'd been asleep for hours. He couldn't believe it was actually morning.

He guessed the other guests had probably gone and that Mr and Mrs Bunn and Henri were either still sleeping or just keeping well out of the way.

Was it really over? Was he really no longer under suspicion?

He thought about how he'd felt when Tiffany had been to his room and brought out his black book and the gold coin. And he'd been forced to reveal the bottle of poison. At that point he had really felt it was all over for him, that the case against him was cemented and he no longer even stood a chance of clearing his name.

Pewter pushed a cup of strong tea towards Seth. 'Hope you slept well. We've spent the last two years after Red Valerian and had not a single lead, just a lot of very unpleasant and suspicious deaths,' Pewter went on, turning back to Marred. 'I've despatched Mr Kingfisher to some people who will be delighted with anything he has to tell us.'

Seth hoped Kingfisher ended up spending a very long time in the same dark cell as Seth had imagined himself in.

'Kingfisher had a ruhnglas, exactly like mine,' explained Seth, his throat raw from where King-fisher had attacked him. 'That's how he got into the dining room with the poison – and put the blame on me. He came prepared.'

He hadn't had the chance to mention he'd discovered Red Valerian's calling card in Kingfisher's room and walked stiffly over to Pewter to wearily hand him the card he'd found and taken from Kingfisher's room. 'I guess this proves he was working for Red Valerian?'

'At least we have our murderer, Boldo, even if the firefly cage may take a little longer,' said Pewter.

'I still don't understand how Kingfisher almost got away with it,' said Count Marred, shaking his head. 'Putting the poison in the dessert like that made it so confusing, so difficult to pin on him. Slippery fellow.'

'Until we get a chance to get the whole truth out of Kingfisher all I can do is offer you my guesses, even though I am sure they are very poor ones,' said Pewter. 'But, for what it's worth, remember – he had the run of the hotel with that ruhnglas and plenty of opportunity for murder. Torpor was really at his mercy.' Pewter sipped his tea thoughtfully. 'I imagine him scouting around for a good opportunity – one that he might get away with and squarely put the blame on someone else. He had arrived armed with poison, we know. He may have planned to do nothing more clever than sneak in on Torpor when he was alone in his bedroom, we may never know. But I can only imagine he must have seen that dessert going into the dining room, all marked up as to only be eaten by Dr Thallomius – well, what would you do? It was an opportunity too good to miss. And a brilliant way to make sure he looked innocent of the crime.'

Seth slumped back on to one of the chairs next to Angelique, who had a black coffee in front of her and was quietly examining the silver top of her red cane.

'The moment Tiffany learnt that all the folk staying in the hotel were magical she would have been desperate to take every chance she got to grab any magic for herself,' said Seth. 'Kingfisher couldn't have known that Tiffany was exactly the sort to completely turn the tables on him the very first moment she got. When Tiffany knew there was a chance to steal an immensely powerful magical device all for herself, she would have seized it. And she quickly did something with it that was terrifying and horrible,' he muttered.

Pewter laid a firm hand on Seth's shoulder. 'The prospect of magic has a very damaging effect on some people.'

'Will she now have magic? The power of that thing?' asked Count Marred.

Seth remembered the lumbering eyeless creatures and knew that wasn't simply bad magic, that was truly terrifying magic.

'We'll have caught up with her before she knows how to control it,' reassured Pewter, checking his ornate wristwatch. 'I'd say there's a 50:50 chance that she'll simply be burnt to a crisp if she tries to use it.'

'And what's the other fifty, Pewter?'

'That she'll end up the most powerful girl in the universe.'

# 50. The Prospect of Magic

Angelique was looking deep into the end of her cane as it glowed blue. Then she snapped the top shut and tapped a shoe against it, giving Pewter a tiny nod.

Pewter turned to the Count. 'We might be on Tiffany's trail quicker than you think. We might have our best lead yet. We should get on to it.'

Did this mean Angelique had managed to take some sort of reading that would give her a clue as to where Tiffany had teleported to? Seth guessed so, but he knew too little about magic to try to understand. Plus he was just too tired.

'Well, that teleport won't stay open for ever,' said Count Marred. 'I should get going.' He said his farewells.

'Am I allowed to know what's going to happen to my book?' asked Seth.

It always seemed to become warm in his hand and belong there. He felt having a connection to a book that presumably had been written by a sinister sorcerer was not a smart thing to admit to. But he suddenly could not bear to think that he'd never see that book again.

Pewter turned from where he was refilling the kettle and his face crinkled into a smile, his eyes shining bright blue behind his glasses. From his pocket, he retrieved the black book and pushed it towards Seth.

Seth reached for it. It was probably the sort of magical artefact Angelique would insist on removing. He quickly tucked it snugly inside his shirt, next to his skin. It glowed.

He looked up to see Angelique standing over him. 'I still don't think you understand,' she said.

'I do. You are an undercover magical secret agent investigating those Missing Feared Exploded. Your job is to discover who actually died in the Unpleasant – and who is in hiding. I even know how you do it – you go into buildings with a known magical history and if there are only traces of old magic, you do things like take away all magical artefacts and it's called "cleaning". See, I know everything. I know that's what brought you here. You were on the trail of Wich Wracht, an MFE, to see if he is alive or dead. Although I still can't believe this Wich Wracht, this sinister sorcerer, used to live here at the Last Chance Hotel. And had Dr Thallomius's firefly cage. It must have been here years. Wich Wracht was a scientific sorcerer and probably conducted all sorts of sinister scientific magic and experiments here. The book is probably his, but if I'm allowed to, I'm going to keep it,' he finished.

Neither Angelique nor Pewter said anything and Seth tried to work out what they weren't telling him.

'The magical history of this place – you're not – you don't mean Mr Bunn is from a magical family?' he asked in horror as more pieces fell together and he really didn't like the picture he was seeing. 'This house—? He just found a way to use the firefly cage, right?' He was struck by an even more terrifying thought. 'Tiffany – she isn't going to inherit magic?'

'You are right that this house is in dire need of

proper cleaning,' sniffed Angelique. 'Goodness knows what a proper clean will find. Magic still in the walls, definitely in the garden. But don't worry, the Bunns aren't a magical family.'

Seth breathed an audible sigh of relief.

Pewter gave out a bark of a laugh. 'Guess you've had enough excitement.' He moved closer to Seth. 'I can see it's nice here. This spooky wood. The glow-worms. The rabbits. What do you know of your heritage, Seth? What did the Bunns tell you about your parents?'

'My father worked for them as a chef and—'

'Seth, you said a moment ago that Wich Wracht ... look, you have worked out that Wich Wracht is a *she*, not a *he*?' said Angelique. 'You do realize that Wich Wracht is quite possibly your mother?'

Seth blinked several times. His mind refused to take in what she was saying. He felt like he might pass out all over again. 'But . . . but Wich Wracht, a sinister MFE, *can't* be m-my mother.'

'It needs proper investigating,' said Angelique. 'But yes, probably.'

That meant Angelique had travelled here to investigate if his *mother* was alive or dead.

It seemed incredible, too much to take in.

Seth delved deep inside his mind for a single

memory of his mother. His father had always become silent or so upset if Seth ever tried to talk about her, he'd stopped a long time ago.

Had she really been a sinister sorcerer and left him a mysterious book that mentioned magical things? What had his father known?

And if his father hadn't ever breathed a word to him about any of that, then what else might there be to learn? What other secrets had his father and his mother been keeping?

His mind ran on. If his mother's official status was Missing Feared Exploded that meant no one was completely sure – was his mother even really dead?

Pewter chuckled. 'And I am pretty sure the Bunns never owned this place. It was your mother's ancestral home. They just took advantage, took it over after your father disappeared, I imagine. You were too young to know what was going on. The Bunns would have got away with it too, if it hadn't been for Miss Squerr and her department checking on these things.' Pewter checked his huge watch. 'OK, duty calls.' He rose.

Seth could only stare from one to the other of them. 'The hotel is *mine*?' He waved around him, looked towards Angelique for confirmation and she was nodding.

'I don't know if you've ever considered the possibility of trying a little magic, Seth?' she said, giving a little cough.

Now this was definitely too much and he could do no more than wordlessly shake his head and feel that his jaw had gone quite slack.

'It's just that there is a possibility, you know, that you could find some sort of spell you could do, even a small one. Just a spark of magic is all you need, you know that. You might try your luck applying for the Prospect and officially join the magical world.'

A huge part of Seth wanted it to be true, that it might really be a possibility. 'I have never done any magic. I'd just be exposed as another of the crackpots out to defraud the magical community,' he whispered. 'Wouldn't I know if I was magic? Inspector Pewter told me that learning magic was one of the most difficult and dangerous skills you could ever undertake. I couldn't even begin—'

'But not for everyone, Seth,' interrupted Angelique. 'Magic is much more complicated than that. Magic, oh it's difficult to explain, magic tends to come differently to different people, and sometimes not at all, even if you really, really want it. I was lucky, I come from a magical family and my inherited magic is really strong. Until you are actually brave enough to try, you won't know if you've inherited any actual magic. It might be really strong like mine. But you'll have to work at it.'

'Or you might be like Miss Troutbean and have inherited none at all,' put in Pewter, turning from where he had reached the door.

Seth thought of the sacrifice Dr Thallomius had made fighting to make sure the magical world stayed strong, for new recruits to be welcomed and nurtured and for sorcerers to use magic for good.

Dr Thallomius had truly believed that anyone could learn and that all you needed was a spark of magic – that and then access to the secret Elysee library of magical texts to train up your magic.

If Angelique thought he had a chance to be admitted to the magical community he would do it. He'd find a way. He'd find a way to be magic.

Only, one thing made him shrink from the idea. If they were right about his mother, and that affinity he had with her black book – did that mean he was destined to do only dark magic?

He made a vow. If he found he did have any magic at all, he'd make sure he never used the sort of magic that led to people dying.

He followed Pewter and Angelique out to the front of the hotel. He'd thought it was going to be difficult to say goodbye, but now he had a mission, he was going to experiment on something even more exciting than recipes, he was going to try to do magic.

'Don't forget, Mr Bunn has some good basic beginners' magical textbooks, Seth,' advised Angelique. 'Give it a try, you might be one of the lucky ones and find it's easier than you think.' She hesitated. 'Only don't use that black book, will you Seth? I expect there are a lot of spells in there, but the difficulty for a beginner is knowing which are the good ones.' She nodded. 'Goodbye Seth.'

Pewter and Angelique were stepping into a shimmering shaft of light that must be their teleport away from the Last Chance Hotel.

'If you promise me you'll try some magic, I promise I'll come back in a couple of weeks and see how you're doing,' shouted Pewter.

'I will!' cried Seth. Would a couple of weeks be enough? Everyone kept telling him how hard magic was. But then it came differently to different people. It was difficult to take it in properly that his mother might have been magic, almost impossible to think he might have inherited her skills.

More than ever, he longed for his parents to be here. Where should he even begin? To even attempt to be like his mother and do magic? He reached out his fingers and twiddled them, as if even knowing there was a chance would make them sparkle with magic like Angelique's cane.

Seth's heart felt easier knowing he would see Pewter again. And the whole of him felt thrilled at knowing the world truly had magic in it, and there was a possibility it might even apply to him. In fact, he itched to go and try it right away as he watched and waved as Pewter and Angelique disappeared.

# ACKNOWLEDGEMENTS

Any journey towards publication needs some hard work, an injection or two of inspiration, and more than just a sprinkling of luck. But what really makes the difference is the friends you make along the way.

So I am fortunate to have many people to thank who have contributed to this book, not least all the goodwill and support I have had from all my family and friends.

Huge thanks to Sally Poyton and Jo Wyton, the most enormously brilliant writers, writing buddies as well as wonderful friends. The rest of my extra-ordinary SCBWI Oxford crit group. We are slowly taking over the world. Everyone I have met through the inspiring Golden Egg Academy and the team at BookBound, you have made such a difference at exactly the right time. Patient readers of early drafts, particularly Elspeth Greig, Sandra Simpson, Alex and Tim Thornton.

I owe a huge thank you to the judges of *The Times/Chicken House Children's Fiction Competition* for choosing my book! And thanks to the whole team at Chicken House who have steered it so expertly through every stage. My book could not have found a happier, talented, more supportive and welcoming home.

Thank you Matt Saunders, illustrator extraordinaire, for making this book such an object of beauty. I really have been extraordinarily lucky.

Thanks to the League of Superheroes, aka the Oxfordshire school librarians – particularly Barbara Hickford and Donna Pocock-Bell – who have shown support, friendship and who tirelessly turn children onto reading, every single day.

And to so many people I know through Mostly Books who made me feel such a complete rock star when I had the news of winning the competition. The greatest bookselling team in the world, Julia Burrows, Sarah Dennis, Catherine Dix, Imogen Hargreaves, Karen Nicholls and Jenna Washington. Not forgetting Graham Jones and other great people in the trade it has been my pleasure to work with. Your support for the book has been incredible.

Finally, none of it would have ever happened without my wonderful and supportive husband, Mark, who has been there the whole journey. Couldn't have done it without you.